HORROR ON ICE

Steed and Purdey looked at the body in the ice-container. The man's chest was opened, his head wrapped in bandages. Purdey gasped: "He's dead."

"Unfortunately not," said the doctor. "He's in a state of suspended animation. Every organ in his body has been kept alive since...an air crash in April, 1945."

The doctor reached forward and pulled the bandages off the man's face. He looked just as he had in his photographs: the cowlick of hair on his forehead, the toothbrush moustache.

"Germany's greatest treasure," Steed said.

From behind them Trasker's voice rasped; "Continue with the operation, Herr Doctor."

THE NEW AVENGERS!

THE NEW AVENGERS 2:
THE EAGLE'S NEST
John Carter

A BERKLEY BOOK
published by
BERKLEY PUBLISHING CORPORATION

First published in Great Britain in 1976
by Futura Publications Limited

Copyright © The Avengers (Film & TV
Enterprises Limited) 1976
Novelisation copyright ©
1976 by Futura Publications Limited

Futura Publications Limited
110 Warner Road
Camberwell, London SE5

SBN 425-03994-3

*BERKLEY MEDALLION BOOKS are published by
Berkley Publishing Corporation
200 Madison Avenue
New York, N. Y. 10016*

BERKLEY MEDALLION BOOK ® TM 757,375

Printed in the United States of America

Berkley Edition, November, 1978

To Sue

Chapter One

John Steed allowed himself a grimace of annoyance as he put the telephone receiver back on the hook. It was a small luxury to allow himself in his disappointment at the call. There came moments when even the coolest of men might momentarily lose their cool and this was one of them. But it was a luxury to be indulged only in private and then only on the rarest of occasions. His eyes wandered regretfully to the sunny view from his study window, then back to the almost empty leather-topped desk— and the small pile of files on one corner of it.

He had been looking forward to a brisk morning's riding. The horse would certainly have enjoyed the outing and so, he hoped, would his latest off-duty companion. Sara was a well-matured lady, who could not have been far off forty, but she combined her maturity and balanced view of the female's role in life with the body and enthusiasm of a woman half her age.

Steed felt that his particular talents would have been well employed on the possibilities offered by such a combination, but, alas, she was to remain, for the moment at least, virgin territory for him. It appeared that her husband, one of those unfortunate appendages with which such a woman is habitually encumbered, was going from his work in Geneva to an equally-profitable deal in New York and had proposed to drop in on his wife for the day—to keep the investment warm, as it were.

Steed got his regrets over quickly. Perhaps there was something in one of the files that would not wait as long as Sara. There was always another day for her.

He reached out reluctantly and pulled the small pile towards him. It consisted of just two thin work-in-progress files and a special 'Your-eyes-only' Memorandum file from 'Mother'. He sighed as he guessed that the latter was probably yet another reminder on cost-effectiveness with particular reference to on-job expenses. The more trivial the communication the greater the secrecy in which it was to be communicated. He decided to get it over with.

The one-sheet memorandum in the file was brief and cold. It announced that an old friend of Steed's, by name Freddy, was being cut adrift from the department for good. There was no more money for him, there were to be no other contacts by members of the department, certainly no pension rights, should he ever reach the age of collecting.

Steed sighed. While Freddy had normally been only involved on the edges of some of the former's larger operations, he had always liked the man and had always hoped that his breakdown would not be a permanent one, that he would one day have been able to go back on to the active list.

It had been over two years since they had last worked together. On that particular job, at a crucial moment of pressure during the bluff and counter-bluff of international espionage, Freddy had lost his nerve. He had subsequently suffered a complete breakdown and had been taken out of the department for a period of rest, which it was planned to be followed by another period as a 'Sleeper'. Most men faced with what Freddy had gone through were back and ready, stronger the second time around, within a year.

For Freddy, it had not worked out quite according to plan. He had found rescue of his own—he had found the bottle and the year's rest produced not a renewed agent, but a weakling alcoholic.

The memo from 'Mother' was only righting the official full stop to what Freddy had done to himself. Steed allowed himself a moment of regret for the passing of a friend, then put the memo aside. He little dreamed how soon it would be before Freddy loomed large in his life. By accident or design, fate had worked out a strange triumph for this failed human being to go out on.

The work-in-progress files were as thin as security and the need for intelligibility would allow. If Steed had his way, there would be no files at all because (a) they were a breach of security in themselves and (b) he hated having to write reports. He and the other members of the department looked upon themselves as men of action rather than pen-pushers. But someone had to keep a check on the broad lines of what was going on, in case of accidents.

Under 'Mother', Steed ran his own little unit, a group of people who worked with him actively, plus a larger group with which he had little personal contact but which carried out routine work such as monitoring, surveillance of sensitive areas and general research. He did need, therefore, to know what everyone was doing—there was always something brewing up in the twilight world that he policed. Most of the brews were stewed—but from a few sprung the adventures that had given him his world-wide espionage reputation.

The two files before him were marked only with their job numbers. He took the higher numbered one first. This was the 'Rostock' file, a long-range, purely speculative excercise. Steed had acquired this operative during the last Government economy drive the year before.

Mottram, who had run the operations of 'Sleeper' surveillance throughout the sensitive areas of the globe since the war, had been swept away. He was old-fashioned in his approach, inflexible, with the result that most of his planted people with their precious and little-used radio sets were in the wrong place.

Steed, backed by 'Mother', who had somehow managed to keep his department intact, moved in to see which of Mottram's operatives it would be of value to maintain and operate. Most had their services dispensed with, but, almost overlooked in the clearout, was a man called Rostock.

He was an engineer who had been sent to the United States to learn aircraft maintenance as part of Lend-lease. Returning to

Russia, he had been already recruited. It had been a godsend to Mottram when he had been banished to Siberia at the end of the war—to run a lumber camp that was almost on the Chinese border. It seemed an odd choice, but then the ways of Papa Stalin were almost as inscrutable as those of Whitehall.

On the face of it, his positioning was too remote to be useful and ripe for closing down. But Steed had one of his famous intuitions and had argued successfully for the man's retention. With the coming of the Sino-Soviet border dispute, Steed, much as usual, had found himself justified.

Until two nights before nothing had been heard from him. It was then that the monitoring office had reported that he had sent through a message. Something big was afoot, something that the Chinese were calling 'Midas'. There had been no more. Rostock had said that he would only send a message again when he had something new to report. So now he was being monitored twenty-four hours a day.

Steed digested all this from the sheet of paper in the file, then picked up a phone and dialled a number. It was answered almost at once and the voice on the line was that of young Morgan, one of the keener of the new operations men. He had joined, keen to be a field operative and would have made a good one, even if he was a little impetuous and overenthusiastic. Unfortunately for him, he had turned out to be an electronics and communication wizard, so he was likely to be stuck on that side for life.

Now his voice came down the wire, 'Morgan, here.'

Steed went through the ritual. 'This is the third son. How is my Mother?'

Morgan snorted. He had little time for all this undercover fiddle-faddle. 'Yes, Mr Steed. How may I help you?'

Steed sighed. 'Morgan, please remember the routine in future. Rostock. You put a note on file. Any clue as to what it's all about.'

Morgan snapped back at once, 'No, sir. There's been a complete radio silence since the message. Nothing further.'

Steed frowned. 'Could he have been wasted?'

'No indication of that, sir. The computer reports the satellite check that the radio's still in position; we know that hasn't been rumbled—so he's not likely to have been.'

4

Steed, too, thought that Rostock's unmasking after thirty years would be unlikely but he forbore to point out to the young man that you didn't have to be caught with a clandestine radio in Siberia to be wasted by the Russian government.

Aloud, he said, 'Thank you, Morgan. I want to know the moment you hear anything, understood?'

He replaced the receiver before the young man had time to reply. Afterwards, he allowed himself one more moment of thought concerning Rostock, before his attention once more wandered out of the window and into the sunshine while he thought about the beautiful ride he was missing.

Regretfully, he retrieved his mind and opened the other file. Again, the information was speculative, but promised more hope of immediate action than had Rostock.

The main object in the file was a large photograph of a distinguished-looking, white-haired, middle-aged man who had been glaring forcefully at the camera when the photograph was taken, as if he regarded the seconds spent on such posing a complete waste of time. In a way it was. He had a face that had recently stared out from the front pages of the world press.

Doctor Maybach von Claus was West Germany's most famous biological scientist. He had spent a lifetime dedicated to research in his field. Now, he was coming to a Society meeting in Britain in a few days time, to unveil the latest results of important research work to the world.

British Intelligence had always had an interest in von Claus and the value of his discoveries to the free world, so the department had decided to cover the man and the lecture.

Steed had selected a young field operative, George Stannard for this apparently simple task. Stannard had at first gone on a routine check of the Doctor's research facilities in West Berlin and, when he had called Steed, what he had to say had put the job into the 'odd' category that 'Mother' hated and that always appealed to the puzzle-solver in Steed. Stannard had been reluctant at first to come straight out with what he had found but, under pressure, he had said, 'Well, you may laugh, but when I was keeping the laboratory under surveillance, I spotted two men doing the same thing.'

Steed had said, 'There's nothing odd about that. Probably

West Berlin security on a routine mission.'

'But this was two monks.'

Steed had smiled into the phone, suddenly awake to the possibilities of the situation. It was the sort of puzzle he liked.

'Any idea where they were from?'

'It was none of the main orders. I'm following up on it now. I'll perhaps go out of town for a few days on it.'

'Well, don't forget you're going to cover the Doctor at his lecture on the eighteenth.'

Those were the last words he had spoken to George Stannard. Steed closed the file and glanced at the digital clock on his desk. It told him that it was the morning of the seventeenth. The Doctor's lecture was due the following day. It might be an idea to call George, just to check he was back and to remind him.

He dialled the number and let it ring nine times. There was no reply. When he replaced the receiver, he was not yet alarmed. George was a reliable man. He would be back from whatever wild goose-chase he had started, to cover the lecture. Of that, Steed could be sure.

The files thus disposed of, Steed turned his attention back to the beauty of the day. He had done quite enough paperwork for one day, as far as he was concerned.

There was no need for him to check his two closest associates, Purdey and Gambit. The former would be getting some well-deserved beauty sleep, while the latter was not due to report back to work until the next day—he was still recovering from two broken ribs he had sustained on their last job. Neither of them would really have to be activated until something concrete happened. The special talents of Steed and his team were always kept in reserve.

In these days of computers and mass communications, such jobs were getting fewer and further between. No one seemed to have the combination of imagination and secretiveness any more. Pushing the thought of Sara that kept coming to the front of his mind, to the back, he speculated that, after the lecture was over, he might even take a few days fishing.

He did not know how close he was to doing so.

● ● ●

When he had left London, fishing had been George Stannard's cover. And Steed would have been alarmed to know it—and to know where he had been going. From a central location in a fishing village on the west coast of Scotland, he had spent a few days travelling through the Islands, looking for a good spot to fish—or to find an obscure order of Scottish monks who wore robes of the distinctive brown that Stannard had seen watching the Doctor's laboratory in Berlin.

It was only the night of the sixteenth that he had found an answer to the question of the location of the order, an answer he might have got if he had bothered to ask on the first night. He was in the bar and the barman said, 'The landlord tells me that you're looking for a good place for some sea angling and that you aren't having any luck?'

Stannard shook his head. 'Not a damned thing.'

'Well, you could try St Dorca, sir. The fishing must be good there.'

Stannard frowned. It was the 'must be' that had caught his attention. 'You make it sound as if you don't know for sure.'

'Well, they don't like too many people on the island.'

'They?'

'The monks, sir.'

'Monks?'

"Yes, sir. The monks of St Dorca. They don't much encourage local visitors there, sir, but they do have foreigners there, like yourself, from time to time. And the fishing must be good, sir. The monks of St Dorca are famous for their fish extract. It goes all over the world.'

Stannard had not publicly wanted to pursue the matter further, but had bidden the barman goodnight after saying that he might locate the island and give it a go sometime in the morning.

He had gone straight to his room and had consulted his maps. Sure enough, the island of St Dorca was marked. Barely seven miles long by five miles wide, it lay off the coast, not twelve miles away. He had gone back through the bar, announcing that he was going for a stroll before turning in. He had gone down to the quay and had hired a small motor-powered boat, getting it gassed up, explaining that he wanted it for an early start in the

7

morning. On the way back to the hotel he got a distinct impression that he was being watched, but there was no evidence with which to back it up. By the time he had regained his room, he put the impression down to an over-active imagination and a sense that he was nearing the end of his search.

He had sat ready in his room at the inn until he was sure that the last of any night-time disturbances had died down. It was nearly three in the morning when he slipped away and down to the quay, carrying the fishing tackle and other gear he felt he might need. At the quay, he untied the boat and rowed it out of the small harbour and beyond the breakwater. Only when he was in open water did he start his engine and set his course for the island. By this simple precaution, and unbeknown to himself, he evaded the close watch that had been put on him from the moment of his chat with the barman.

From his check of his maps, he already knew that the island had, facing the mainland, one small village. To the north of this stood the monastery and its grounds, while a number of crofters' cottages dotted around made up the only other habitation. The south end of the island seemed deserted and so it was to the south that he made his way under cover of the welcome darkness.

To reach the beaches on the south side, he had to pass close to a rocky headland. Beyond it was a beach, wide and gently sloping to the cliffs of a headland. He switched off his motor and allowed the boat to beach itself. With his gear he then walked along the soft sand until he reached a point where the headland sloped gently down to the beach, as if to greet the great Atlantic rollers. From here it was open sea all the way to the coast of North America.

Stannard had already decided that his best plan of campaign was to go up the Atlantic coast of the island, making a casual survey, thus approaching the monastery from the north, still unobserved. His fishing equipment gave him a back-up in case his presence was observed and anyone should question him.

He struck out north, carefully circling the cottages he saw in the dawn light and, by full daylight, he had made most of the distance that he wanted to cover. At last he reached a headland that formed the northern tip of the island and began to climb to the lip so that he might get a view, if he could, of the monastery and the village to the south of him. As he climbed over the springy heather, he could hear the breakers smashing against great rocks below, and grinned. There would certainly be no fishing there.

Half way up the slope he got the first intimation that he was not alone, and turned abruptly. Two men had appeared and were standing a distance away to one side of him. From the direction in which they had come it was more than reasonable to suppose that they had been deliberately tracking him for some time. Both men, like himself, held fishing rods, as if out for a day's sport, but something about the way that they were holding the rods and standing and watching him made him immediately aware that they represented imminent, if inexplicable, danger.

Neither of the men was more than thirty years of age but of the two, the elder was dark-haired, the younger blond and nordic-looking. The elder man turned to his companion and nodded. The other man immediately prepared his rod as if to make a cast.

George Stannard took all this in during the few seconds in which he faced them, glued to the spot. As the second man also prepared his rod for a cast George galvanised himself into action. Dropping his own equipment, he turned and ran up the headland, then dodged away to make a run in the general direction of the monastery and the village.

Behind him there came a sudden whistling sound in the air as the first of the men cast his line, then something plucked at the sleeve of his anorak before falling away. A second whistle produced a second tug at the anorak, this time at the shoulder. He glanced down to see a tear in his sleeve, knew at once there would be another in the shoulder and came to the bizarre but undeniable conclusion that the men were using their lines on him—that he was the big fish they were out to catch. He forced his pace down the slope of the hillside.

There was a dip, then he came to a rise and slewed round as he reached the summit. The two men were following, but more slowly as they reeled in and prepared their lines for another cast. By the time he was plunging down from the rise, there came the same whistle of the lines through the air and once more the hooks found their marks, this time on the back of his outer garments. If fishing was their real profession, these men were experts in their field.

He could see the monastery now, nestling in the dale below him. The stone buildings covered a wide area and a thin plume of smoke from one of the larger buildings told him that they were in use. He started down the hillside towards the buildings and, even as he did so, he heard the monastery bell start to toll, loud and slow, the sound drifting up the hillside.

Half way down, he glanced round and saw the two men reeling in their lines on the brow of the slope. He redoubled his efforts to get away from them before they would be ready to cast afresh.

The younger of the two men turned to his companion and said in an English accent that was just too good to be true, 'Shall I go ahead after him, Main?'

'No, Ralph. We can afford to take our time.'

Matching deed to word he began to stroll down the slope towards the monastery buildings, taking the same route as the fugitive. Stannard was almost at the buildings now. One burst of speed and he had reached them. The bell tolled out loudly now, as if guiding him in to safety.

Inside the Great Hall of the monastery, monks were assembling for a meeting called by the bell. They entered the huge, vaulted hall from corridors that led from the wings of the building. At one end of the hall there were a pair of heavy, studded doors and the men lined up in ranks facing them. When most of them were in their places, one of the doors opened, a man entered and the door quickly closed behind him. The newcomer was older than most of the others, though, like them, he wore the simple brown habit of the order. But, while those before him had the shaved pates that are a feature of monastic life, their leader had a full mane of thick white hair.

A hush fell on the assembled men and they looked up expectantly to the newcomer. He stepped forward, both arms raised in a gesture that was a mixture of greeting and blessing.

'Welcome, my brothers. A blessing upon you all. As you all know, we are but a few days away from...'

There came the sound of commotion in one of the entrance doorways that led to the outside of the building and the man stopped abruptly. Some of the monks turned in the direction of the noise, then faced front again as the old man started to speak once more, in a louder voice, to keep their attention.

'My brothers, please. I was telling you that we are but a few days away from the most auspicious event in our annual calendar—April the twentieth, and I must ask you...'

Once more he broke off. The hubbub had become louder and now, pushing his way through the assembly, came George Stannard, his anorak torn, his eyes wild with fear. He glanced over his shoulder as he pressed through the lines of men before falling on his knees in front of their leader, struggling for breath, so that he might speak.

The old man looked down at him with a passive benevolence, before asking, 'What may we do for you, my son?'

Stannard struggled for breath. 'Sanctuary...'

The old man frowned and Stannard, his breath returning, repeated, 'Sanctuary, Father. I seek sanctuary.'

Still the old man leaned forward, not replying.

'Please, Father, I beg you—'

The words were cut short in his throat as the familiar whistling sound came through the air and the fishing line curled round his neck, choking him. The rod jerked and he was asprawl on the stone floor of the great room, his hands clutching at his throat as he gasped for air.

The rows of monks had parted and now Main and Ralph stepped through them. It was Main's line which had caught the fugitive and as he stood over his captive, he gave a little bow to the Father, who was regarding him mildly.

'Please forgive us Father Trasker. It is but a small matter that need not concern you here. Please go on about your business.'

The old man nodded, remaining quite still as the two hunters bent over their victim, taking an arm each and jerking him to his feet. They turned him and half-dragged, half-walked him through the hall, the monks standing aside for them. They headed for one of the exits and, as the doors closed on them, the last words that the dazed and frightened Stannard heard were

11

from the old Abbot, words spoken as if nothing had happened.

'My brothers. The twentieth of April is one of the most important dates in our calendar...'

Stannard was in a long corridor. The walls were of whitewashed stone and, set in at intervals, were plain but obviously heavy wooden doors. The floor was of stone but the whole impression was one of well-lit airiness.

His captors stopped abruptly at one of the wooden doors. It was bolted on the outside and Main held Stannard up while Ralph slipped back the bolts and pushed the door open. Then he rejoined Main, holding the captured man's arms, while the older man carefully unwound the line that had been cutting into the flesh of Stannard's neck.

He was pushed into the tiny room beyond the door and fell heavily to the stone floor. He heard the door slam behind him and the sound of the bolts being pushed home. As he picked himself painfully up and glanced round, he saw that he was completely trapped.

He found himself in a tiny monk's cell. He had never been in a monastery before, but the cell looked almost identical to cells depicted in the cinema or on television.

The floor was bare. In one corner stood a rudimentary bed, above it a cross, next to it a low table on which stood an empty candle holder. The only other piece of furniture in the room was a plain wooden chair. Light was supplied by a long, Medieval slit in one wall, too narrow for even the thinnest of children to slip through.

George Stannard tried to stare out through the slit, but could see nothing beyond it but another stone wall. He slumped down on the bed to sort out his thoughts and to consider his next move. As he went over the events of the morning he rubbed at his neck which was sore from where the line had cut into the skin.

It seemed that his visit had opened up a nest of vipers—but he was unable to puzzle out what sort of nest. There still seemed to be no connection between a lonely monastery on an island in the West of Scotland, occupied by monks of an obscure order and Germany's leading biologist. There was certainly something strange about the two men who had captured him, about their voices, their precise English. The strange behaviour of the

Abbot and monks, this troubled him too. Then there was the Abbot himself and his reiteration of the date: the twentieth of April. Stannard was not a deeply religious man but he knew enough to know that the twentieth of April was not a particularly special day in the Church calendar.

Somehow, he knew that the date had a significance that was involved in his capture, but for the life of him he could not make a connection that carried any conviction in his own mind.

Stannard did not have much time to work his thoughts into any sort of order to provide a theory as to what was going on. In the corridor, he heard the sound of hurrying footsteps on the stone flags and the murmur of voices. They stopped immediately opposite his door and the bolts were drawn back. When the door opened, it was Main and Ralph who strode into the room first, but a newcomer followed hard on their heels.

He was a tall, thick-set man of about sixty. His hair was cut short in a vaguely military fashion. His blue, nordic eyes had the hardness of diamonds. George Stannard recognised the look in them. He had seen faces and eyes like that among the prisoners who had once been the members of the SS elite—the Gestapo. He could detect the trace of an accent in the man's voice as he snapped, 'Has he been searched?'

It was Main who answered, 'No, sir. We waited for you.'

'Do it now.'

As Main and Ralph moved towards him, Stannard tried to rise to fend them off. He was still weak from his long run and the ordeal of capture and they took him as easily as a baby, ramming him down into the hard chair, so that the back of his head hit the back of the chair with a loud crack and a searing pain shot through his head. Momentarily stunned, he offered little further resistance as the men went through his pockets with a practised ease that showed they were professionals.

By the time the pain had gone and his eyes were back in focus, his wallet and papers were in the newcomer's hands. There was a silence in the cell as the man went through his papers and Stannard shouted into it, 'You can't get away with this.'

The newcomer smiled at the cliché. 'You English are so predictable. We have got away with it and we will, be sure of that.'

13

Something among Stannard's papers engaged his full attention and he placed the rest of the things on the edge of the bed before holding it up. To the uninitiated it looked like just another credit card—but it was, in fact, Stannard's special security clearance, a card carried by all of the operatives in 'Mother's' department. His antagonist was obviously among the initiated.

'Well, well. Mr George Stannard. How do you do. You are on a fishing holiday, I understand?'

Although George knew that he had been rumbled he tried to maintain his cover.

'Yes. I've been touring along the coast.'

The man shook his head with mock regret. It reminded George of the 'This will hurt me more than it hurts you' schoolmasters that had tyrannised his childhood.

'That really isn't good enough, Mr Stannard. You're on more of a fishing expedition than a fishing holiday. For the latter it would hardly be necessary for you to carry a top British Intelligence Security card, would it?'

In spite of the strong hands holding him, George managed a shrug. 'I need that for my job. Shouldn't have brought it away with me really.'

The man leaned forward. 'And what exactly is your job, Mr Stannard?'

'I'm a decoding clerk at the Foreign Office.'

The man shook his head and tapped the card impatiently against the knuckles of his other hand. 'Come, now, Mr Stannard. You can do better than that. Why don't you try again. No one in the Foreign Office needs a clearance as high as this.'

Well, so much for his cover story. Stannard did not answer, but tried to stare his questioner down. The other man averted his eyes first, affording Stannard a small victory. Then he said, 'Help him with his answer.'

George was helpless to avoid the persuasion of the two men who held him. Main grabbed him by his still-sore neck and cracked his head back against the crossbar of the chairback. At the same time, Ralph's bunched fist crashed into his rib-cage, causing him to wince with pain. He tried to relax under a hail of blows and, as they ceased abruptly at a word of command from his interrogator, he slumped forward in the chair, before being pulled upright again.

'Come now, Mr Stannard. Let's try again. Who do you work for?'

He gasped, 'I told you before.'

'We know that's a lie. I have very little more patience. Who do you work for?'

'The Foreign Office—a coding clerk.'

'Mr Stannard, please. You have a special security clearance. We know that means you have to be working for one of the British Intelligence departments—we just need to know which one.'

George found an inner reserve of calm. Things were not necessarily as black as they appeared. The men who held him did not have all the answers and this obviously frightened them. That was why it was so important for them to know. Perhaps they would end up giving more away than they learned.

'I am waiting for your answer, Mr Stannard.'

He looked at the older man and shook his head. 'You've had all the answers you're getting from me.'

The man nodded at the two men who were holding Stannard and they went to work on him again. He felt the salt taste of blood in his mouth as they hit him repeatedly. At last, when he was dazed enough to believe that he was slipping into unconsciousness, he was held upright again and the interrogator stepped forward, thrusting the identity card under his nose.

'Mr Stannard, you surely will not deny further what I have told you about yourself. You will be able to spare yourself a great deal of further pain if you will just tell us who sent you.'

George managed a weak smile. 'It was the barman at my hotel, actually. He said the fishing was good.'

The man held his temper in check, then shrugged. 'Suppose I were to say that I believed you. Would it make any difference now? Would it change your fate?'

George took a deep breath. He knew exactly what the man was implying—and the truth of it. He was a dead man at their hands whether they believed him or not. He kept silent and the man snapped, 'Main, you will deal with him.'

This time, George Stannard was ready for his two

tormentors. As they turned to begin working him over afresh, he rose suddenly from his chair and kicked forward, catching the interrogator in the pit of the stomach and propelling him back against the wall. His head hit the stone with a sickening thud and he slipped down to the floor, no longer taking an interest in the proceedings.

Having eliminated one third of his opposition, he set about the other two. His sudden movement had caught the two men off balance and they had crashed into one another. He turned abruptly as they regained their balance, grabbed their heads and banged them together. Main tottered and he fell as Ralph crashed on top of him.

Giving them no time to argue with the referee's decision, George turned, sprang over the fallen body of their comrade and made for the door, slamming it shut behind him as he went. It was the work of a moment to push the well-oiled bolts home and that temporarily took care of the first wave of the opposition.

He glanced up and down the corridor, making sure that there was no one else around, then sprinted off in the opposite direction to the way he had been brought, hoping that he would find a doorway that would lead him out of the monastery to the comparative freedom of being on the run. Behind him he could hear shouts and the sound of fists against the bolted door. It could not be long before they were free and in pursuit, with the alarm sounded.

There was a bend in the corridor and he disappeared round it not a moment too soon. A monk emerged from one of the other cells, attracted by the noise that the imprisoned men were making and drew back the bolts. Main and Ralph spilled out, pushing past him and looking up and down the corridor.

The older man was up on his knees and shouted after them, 'Sound the alarm—and make sure you get him. He must not leave the island alive.'

At the end of the corridor a door stood ajar. Stannard made his way cautiously towards it and saw that it led out on to what must once have been the stable yard of the complex of buildings that made up the monastery. It seemed deserted and he stepped out, moving slowly at first, then at top speed to cross to the archway that led him out to open countryside.

A distance away to the south was a belt of trees. They would provide him with cover and he raced for them. Once in the trees, he took his bearings. His best bet was to make for the village to see if he could steal a boat from the quay. If that proved impossible he could always go on. There was a chance that his own little boat had not been found.

He started off through the trees and the bushes that lay beyond them. Behind him, he heard the monastery bell start to peal, louder and with a more urgent note than before. Stannard redoubled his speed, crouching low, trying to take as much advantage of the cover as he could. Soon he was on a hillside overlooking the sleepy fishing village. All seemed quiet enough, but he had had enough bad experiences on the island that morning to make him wary of the illusion of peace.

Beyond the cluster of fisherman's dwellings, an inn and a small row of shopfronts, was the quay—and tied to it a number of fishing boats. Stannard came slowly down the hill, circling the village and keeping in cover, making his way as close as he could to the quay without entering the village itself. He came under these precautions to a point where he could hear the water lapping against the quay in the silence that was all round. The sound of the monastery bell floating in on the wind was the only other noise he could hear. The village seemed almost unnaturally deserted.

He moved forward slowly and cautiously. He was almost on the quay when he spotted one of the hidden men. He was crouched down in one of the boats. He turned and ran back towards cover, away from the village and to the south.

All at once the quay and the village erupted into life. It was as if they had all hidden themselves in a trap for him. A man ran to the end of the quay and began to ring the fog-warning bell. George ran for his life, with his new pursuers on his tail.

He spent the next hour moving progressively closer and closer to his own beached boat. His pursuers were sweeping south after him, but, covering a large area in their search, they were well behind. He could only pray that he had not been outflanked by any of his pursuers from the monastery. They must not be waiting for him when he got to his boat.

In front of him was the slope of the headland that overlooked the southern beach. He ran up it over the springy heather, then found he had chosen the wrong spot—where the cliff was highest. He turned to go down the slope and saw that a group of villagers had reached the bottom and were starting up after him.

He turned to move away from them and saw that Main was already blocking this line of escape, his fishing rod in his hands, a look of grim concentration on his face.

Stannard was left with only one way to go. He turned and glanced down towards the beach. It seemed an awful long way down. Out of the corner of his eye, he could see Main getting ready to make his cast. As the line started to whistle forward, he jumped out and down into space, falling like a stone. The line whistled over his head harmlessly. He tried to relax his body against the moment of impact, to lessen the chances of putting himself out of action on landing. The drop looked steep enough to break every bone in his body.

The shock when he hit the ground was the opposite of what he expected—as he fell into loose sand. It was like landing on a feather mattress. At the last moment, however, he fell forward and winced as he felt his ankle give. It hurt as he freed it from the sand and he found his foot was dragging as he started across the beach to where he could still see his boat, beached but apparently untouched.

As he went, he glanced upward and saw the villagers on the headland above him, not daring to make the jump themselves. There was no sign of Main in their midst. He glanced down the beach, but the man had not appeared.

He turned his attention back to his main chance—getting to the boat and making his getaway. On the headland, the villagers turned and started down the slope to come to the point where they could get on the beach at no danger to themselves—which would place them farther away from the fugitive and his transport than they were at present. As for Main, he carefully reeled in his line and took a route of his own. There was no need to chase the fugitive. Stannard would be coming to him, of that he was certain. His line was made ready for another cast, with Main taking care not to touch the unbarbed hook on the end of the line.

His ankle throbbing, Stannard entered the water and waded

18

along the edge of the tide until he reached the boat. If he had ever felt like praying, this was the moment.

He pulled the string of the starter motor. For a moment, the cold engine seemed about to catch and come to life—then it died. He let the starter snap back, then checked the petrol lead and tried again. Once more the motor fired, then spluttered out. He had taken precious moments, there would be little time left for other chances.

Some of the men had reached the beach now and were running towards him through the sand. Time was getting very short indeed, but this sort of engine was not something that could be rushed into work in an emergency. It would take its own time.

Stannard quickly checked over the motor, then made what he knew would have to be a last try. This time the motor coughed, caught, started to splutter, then caught again, revving hard.

He pushed the boat off the sand and jumped in as it began to float out into deeper water, before revving up and steering himself away from the shore. He was not a moment too soon as the villagers reached the water's edge. The more enthusiastic of them waded out after him, let the water get as far as their waists, then stopped. They all fell behind him as he gathered speed and set out for the mainland. The closest he would come to the island again would be in navigating his way round the rock headland that stood between him and his straight run home.

It was as he approached the channel, south of the rocks, that he saw that danger still threatened him. Main had walked out as far as he could on the rocks and was standing waiting. There was a look approaching triumph on his face as he stood, rod ready for the cast, just waiting for the little boat to get close enough.

From previous experience, Stannard had no reason to believe that Main would miss with his cast. Fear threw bile into his throat and he tried to work out how he could avoid the other man's line. He put his hands up to protect his neck, for he worked out that the man could only really endanger him if the line went round his throat as it had in the Great Hall of the monastery.

Main waited until the little boat was level with him and only then did he make his cast. The line curved out, whistling threateningly through the air. The unbarbed hook flicked forward and touched Stannard's cheek, before Main began to reel in quickly as if preparing himself for another cast.

Stannard could see that the smirk of triumph was still on the man's face. He put his hand up to where the hook had touched his cheek and felt the tiny smear of blood.

It seemed that Main's last try for him had been a pointless gesture. The boat moved on into open water and he steered it straight for the mainland. He glanced back and saw that Main was still there, watching him go.

He felt himself out of danger now. With the villagers having chased him to the southern tip of the island, it would be a while before they could get back and put boats out after him. There was no sign that they had already done so. He could be on the mainland before they had even got their boats underway. Once there, a quick call to Steed would ensure that the area would be swarming with police. Whatever secrets the islanders were protecting would be secrets no more.

He realised that he was feeling hot in spite of the cold spring breeze that was blowing off the sea. He passed his hand across his forehead and it came away covered in a sweat that was as cold as he was warm. He put it down as reaction to his exertions in getting away. Then the first wave of dizziness came over him.

Stannard steadied himself against the side of the boat and shook his head to clear the muzziness. It was nothing, merely fatigue. It had been a long night and day and it was far from over. His chest, face and stomach were still aching from the beating he had taken, his throat was sore and his damaged ankle throbbed angrily.

Again the wave of dizziness swept over him and this time he could hear a muffled buzzing in his ears. He felt himself start to fall, concentrated all his efforts into staying upright and the dizziness receded, the buzzing almost ebbing away. His legs seemed suddenly weak and the small nick on his cheek throbbed with renewed pain.

As he went dizzy for the third time, he realised what had happened to him and the reason for Main's smile of triumph. The hook had been spiked with a special bait all its own—a bait that killed. He turned and saw the still figure of his murderer silhouetted against the sky, motionless on the rocks, looking out across the water at him.

Stannard turned away. It was the last conscious move he made. The blackness came over him like a wave and he slumped down in the boat. He was dead almost before he fell.

The boat and its dead passenger moved away from the island, further out in the channel towards the mainland. Main allowed himself the luxury of a second smile, before carefully reeling in his line, making sure that he did not touch the unbarbed hook that had carried the poison. Then he turned and began to clamber over the rocks and back to the shore. The motor-boat would soon run out of fuel driving unattended and it might drift for days before it was found. Three days was all the islanders needed and he had more than bought it for them.

That night, there was a meeting at the monastery. Main was one of those who attended, as were Ralph and Gunner, the young monk who had unlocked the door of the cell and given the alarm.

The fishermen had gone out and searched for the motorboat that afternoon on the orders of Stannard's interrogator, but they had come up with nothing. This man, Karl, now chaired the meeting and while he reported disappointment that the body had not been found, he did not think that the day had gone entirely wrong.

'At the very least, gentlemen, we have had a certain amount of good fortune.'

The old man sitting at the table snapped, 'In what way, Karl.'

'This, sir.'

So saying, he held up the dead man's wallet. He opened it and produced a piece of notepaper as well as the identity card.

'This piece of paper tells us that our Mr George Stannard, which ever service he works for, was assigned to cover the von Claus lecture. We have his order paper and his identity card—which should save us an awful lot of trouble.'

Ralph laughed: 'I can take it a bit easier, then.'

'It is indeed one job less for you, Ralph. But you will still need the clothes from his apartment to wear, in case.'

The old man at the table leaned forward. 'Do you think, perhaps we should exercise just a little caution. I mean—well, he could have been sent here deliberately, as only part of a team.'

Karl shrugged. 'What if he was? They can't really know anything or they'd have sent more than one man. Anyway, when he doesn't report in, they'll mount a search for him. By the time they have found him along this coast it will be too late.'

The man at the head of the table thought for a moment, then nodded, 'You are right, Karl. You usually are. Anyway, the risk must be taken. We have to be ready for the twentieth of April— we have to be . . .'

Chapter Two

John Steed took his anger off the boil by driving from his home to the block that contained Stannard's apartment rather faster than perhaps he ought to have gone. The journey satisfied him, but left a series of nervous drivers in his wake.

He slowed down and turned the car off the road into the car park that fronted on the apartment block where Stannard lived. He was puzzled that he had once more not been able to get George on the phone that morning. As an operative he had less imagination than Steed's closest collaborators, but he was a man who had proved utterly reliable. Now, with the German Doctor's lecture only a matter of a few hours away, it should have been possible to reach him. But he was not answering his phone.

So, this morning, it had been Steed's turn to cancel a riding appointment with Sara. He was beginning to think that he would never get close to the damned woman and it dented his otherwise well-polished ego.

He slid into a space in front of the block, just behind a large, black Mercedes and jammed on the brakes. When he jumped out, his bowler hat was at a rakish angle, his umbrella dangling from one careless hand. John Steed was ready for anything.

He hardly glanced at the Mercedes as he went through the glass doors and crossed the deserted lobby to the lift. It was on the ground floor and he stepped easily inside, using the ferrule of his umbrella to press the button for the sixth floor on which Stannard lived.

He was not the first visitor that the late George Stannard had been blessed with that morning. Ralph had arrived first in the big black Mercedes, shortly ahead of Steed and even now he was changing into Stannard's clothes in the sixth-floor apartment. It had given him much ironic pleasure to see, in the dead man's living-room, a silver framed photograph of a fishing expedition in the West Indies. Stannard was standing next to a huge marlin he had caught. So, that part of his story had had a certain truth to it. Perhaps he really had only visited St Dorca on a fishing trip.

He had left the front door slightly ajar so that he could hear anyone approaching from the lifts or the corridor and now he was hurriedly stuffing the pockets of his stolen suit with the dead man's personal effects. If anything should go wrong at the lecture and he should be caught or killed the authorities could only prove that he was impersonating George Stannard.

He was almost ready when he heard first the arrival of the lift then a door to another flat along the corridor opening and closing. Hurriedly he checked that he had all he needed for his mission. Then he made his preparations in case one of the people moving about on the floor was making their way to Stannard's flat.

Steed came out of the lift, his umbrella resting on his shoulder. Half way along the corridor, a door opened and a little old lady appeared. She was about seventy years old and looked to Steed just like everyone's maiden aunt.

She came down the corridor towards him, her hands vaguely fluttering in front of her, a smile on her face. Steed stood aside and let the umbrella fall to his side as his free hand went to the brim of his bowler in a polite gesture.

The old lady came abreast of him so that between them they blocked the corridor. She paused and turned, looking him up and down for a second, as if either wishing she was thirty years younger—or deciding whether he was gentleman enough to be spoken to without a formal introduction. Then, deciding that he was mature and steady enough, she said, 'You haven't seen my Posey-poof?'

Steed froze in disbelief. 'Your what?'

'My Posey-poof.'

Steed raised his hat and shook his head. 'Madam, I am widely travelled. I would even admit to being, in my own small way, a man of the world. But I don't think I'd know a Posey-poof if it jumped up and bit me.'

It seemed that, by accident, he had said the right thing. The woman beamed and fluttered her hands dangerously close to Steed's face. 'Oh, my Posey-poof never bites, oh, dear, no.'

Steed divined at last that Posey-poof was the old lady's dog.

'Never? He must indeed be a very well-disciplined creature.' He tried to get past, but in vain.

'Oh, dear, no, he never does. I was just going to take him for walkies. I must have left the door open just a teeny bit—and he was gone.'

Steed was becoming impatient, but, as was his usual rule, he tried not to show it to the old lady.

'I see, so the little tyke has got away—I mean, wandered off for a moment. Well, if I find him, I'll bring him straight back, I can promise you that, madam.'

'Dear boy.'

He took this as a blessing, replaced his hat and moved on. As he went to Stannard's door, he muttered, 'Posey-poof, oh my God.'

As he got to the door, he stopped abruptly, realising that it was not shut properly. It was too late to exercise caution now. Anyone inside would have heard him talking in the corridor with the old lady. He raised his hand and rapped on the door, shouting, 'Stannard? George?'

Ralph was crouched ready, behind the door. Steed knocked a second time, got no reply and pushed open the door.

'George?'

Even as he spoke and took a pace forward into the room, Ralph kicked up hard against the door. It slammed back, hit Steed on the shoulder and pushed him off-balance across the room. Ralph jumped over him and went fast down the corridor.

It took Steed a couple of seconds to get back on to his feet and give chase.

Luck was on Ralph's side. The old lady was at the lift and had just pressed the button that had summoned it. The lift doors were open and Ralph ran down the corridor towards it. Steed caught up with him just outside the lift and managed to get one hand on his shoulder. Then something jerked at his feet and he fell heavily, crashing to the ground.

In the seconds that followed Ralph was in the lift and the doors closed on his felled pursuer.

Steed glanced down at what trapped him and saw that his foot was caught up in the loop of a dog's lead. While he struggled to his feet, trying to disentangle himself, the old lady fluttered up to him.

'Oh, what a nice, clever man. You've found my little Posey-poof. I knew you would.'

Steed managed to get up and disentangled. The old woman was blocking his way to the lift and he heard the whirr of it starting to descend. The indicator above it traced its rapid descent. The old lady prattled on.

'I'm sure you wouldn't mind lifting him up for me—it's my back, you know.'

Steed, kindness still near his heart, in spite of a desire to take the little old lady and her dog and throw them down the lift shaft, scooped up the dog, though the frown on his face showed he was still intent on finding some way of following Ralph.

The woman took the animal from him, but still managed somehow, in spite of her frail appearance, to block the way to the lift.

'Oh, I cannot tell you how grateful I am. Posey is my only company, you know.'

Steed gritted his teeth as the lights on the indicator flashed at the first floor. 'Madam...'

'All I can do is offer you a cup of tea by way of thanks.'

The lift indicator showed that the fugitive had reached the ground floor. Steed didn't stand a chance now. He sighed and moved back down the corridor, the old lady in his wake.

'Madam, it would be a pleasure to take tea with you. But it will have to be some other time, may I?'

He opened her door for her and ushered her in as if he were going to follow. She stopped in the doorway.

'Thank you, young man. You have made an old lady very happy.'

Steed doffed his bowler, waited until she had moved into her apartment far enough, then quickly shut the door, leaving himself on the outside. He then turned and dashed like mad into George Stannard's apartment. He crashed his way across the living-room and made for the window from where he could look down into the car park. He was in time to see the large black Mercedes speeding away.

Steed went quickly through the apartment, cursing himself and the old lady for the delay that had made him too late to catch a glimpse of the number plate of the car. There was no sign of George Stannard anywhere in the apartment. All the signs showed that he had left in an orderly manner, as if going away for a few days. The only oddities were a fisherman's jersey, trousers and boots in a pile on the floor of the bedroom.

Steed slumped down in a living-room chair, his mind working furiously. Then he came to a decision. With the stranger in Stannard's apartment and the latter's disappearance, the covering of Dr von Claus had moved from the 'unusual' to being a living mystery. It was time to call in Gambit and Purdey. He reached out for the phone.

Gambit was on the floor of his apartment, doing some setting-up exercises when the phone began to ring. He swore, got up and crossed the room in quick, easy strides. Gambit was in his thirties, darkly handsome and in lithely athletic condition. To Steed he was the perfect fighting machine—a tuned body attached to a brain that worked with almost computer-like speed. He was particularly useful for jobs that Steed found just a little too energetic to go with his image and dress sense.

On the desk was a modern phone with an amplified talkback device attached to it. Gambit leaned across the desk and picked up the receiver, putting it in the amplifier. He hoped it was Steed at the other end, Steed always hated talking over it. He smiled as he heard his boss's voice.

'Gambit.'

'Yes.'

'Gambit. It's Steed. I want Purdey.'

Gambit laughed. 'Who doesn't.'

Steed's oath was amplified by the machine and he bit off each word with studied patience. 'Purdey is not answering her phone—and you live just round the corner from her.'

'Okay, there's no need to rub it in. Where are you?'

'Stannard's apartment.'

'George Stannard? Where is he?'

Steed snapped, 'That's what we've got to find out.'

'Purdey and I will be there post-haste.'

Purdey lived in a comfortable mews cottage just round the corner from Gambit's airy apartment. In spite of her comparative late induction into the security services, Steed had found her as reliable and mentally alert a companion as any he had had before. In the elegance and beauty department she came well up to standard as well. She was, however, much more liberated than even Mrs Peel had been and her relationship with her co-workers depended as much on their loyalty as her own. She was, in short, a new liberated woman, though, in her case, none the worse for such liberation.

Gambit approached the cottage and saw that all the curtains were still drawn in spite of the fact that it was well past eleven. Gambit went to the door, then stood as if he had just rung the bell and was waiting for the occupant to answer the front door. In truth, the free hand that his body covered was working away with a useful piece of wire that he always kept on his person and, seconds later, the lock clicked and he slipped inside without a sound.

The downstairs rooms showed some evidence of a recent party and he went quickly up the stairs to the master bedroom of the little house. He opened the bedroom door to be greeted by a blackness that was only partially alleviated by a crack in the curtains.

He glanced quickly round the room. On a bedside table, the phone was buzzing gently, having been taken off the hook. Next to the phone, incongruously, sat a Hookah and a pair of ballet shoes. On two small tables, two chess games were laid out, one of them already in progress, the other one yet to begin. There was a pile of the latest fashion magazines on the floor and, on the wall, a collection of valuable fob watches. A chair was laden with fashionably elegant, if creased, clothing.

The central object of the room was the large bed. In the centre of this, under the covers, was a huddled mass that had to be Purdey overdoing her beauty sleep.

Gambit smiled and moved silently into the room. He got to the edge of the bed, then, with a sudden movement, he tipped the mattress up on to the floor, at the same time shouting, 'Good morning.'

He went quickly over to to curtains and opened them, letting the sunlight stream in. He turned round, just a fraction of a second too late. Purdey was sitting up amid the disarranged covers, but she had already draped her obvious nudity in the sheets. He grinned down at her confusion, crossed past her and put the phone back on the hook.

'Good morning, Purdey. I'm sorry if I woke you, but we don't seem to be answering our phone. Duty calls.'

She was still too shocked by his familiarity to have gathered her wakening thoughts, and he went on, 'There's neither the need nor the time for you to look at me like that. I tipped you out of bed—not into it.'

She sniffed. 'The main trouble with you is that you were weaned from your prep school too early.'

He merely shrugged and she slumped down again. 'Good-night, Gambit.'

He sighed. 'Come on, Purdey.'

'Oh, shut up. I need my beauty sleep.'

Gambit snorted. 'No. There's a lot of things you do need and I'd like to discuss it with you some other time. But that isn't one of them—definitely.'

'Mike Gambit—one of these days...'

He chuckled. 'I know. I'm looking forward to it.'

She struggled to her feet, keeping the sheets draped modestly round her tall, slim figure. 'Is it Steed?'

'Yes.'

'Any idea what it's about?'

'George Stannard.'

29

Purdey frowned. 'But I thought he was one of our operatives. What's happened to him?'

'That's what Steed would like to know. Get dressed, Purdey. It sounds like one right up our street.'

Purdey smiled. 'Whether it is or it isn't, you can wait for me downstairs.'

'This once, just to oblige.'

He left the room. Purdey got ready and dressed quickly. She was tall and slim, with long blonde hair and legs that never seemed to end. It took her only a few minutes to dress and apply her make-up, and by the time she went down the stairs she looked as if she had been getting herself ready for hours. Gambit could not suppress a smile of admiration.

She said, 'I feel suicidal. You can drive.'

They went out to the powerful car that stood at the kerb. A few minutes of death-defying driving from Gambit and they were sliding into the space behind Steed's car where the black Mercedes had been parked.

They went up to the sixth floor in silence. Purdey rang the bell and it was Steed who answered the door. He looked unruffled in spite of his recent experience.

'Come in. It would seem we have a little mystery on our hands.'

'What's happened to George Stannard?' Purdey asked.

'Well, he seems to have disappeared.'

'Disappeared?'

Steed sighed. 'Why don't you both sit down and I'll give you a quick run-down.'

He waited until the other two were settled. 'Now, fact. Mother reported that it had been drawn to his attention that a Doctor Mayback von Claus was going to give a lecture in a private institution on his biological surgery techniques. Mother felt that we ought to cover the lecture. I assigned George Stannard. It didn't seem like a strenous assignment at the time. The lecture is today, this afternoon in fact.'

Purdey interrupted. 'It all seems quite straightforward to me.'

Steed nodded. 'It was—until George disappeared.'

'Disappeared?'

'Yes. I tried to call him yesterday and again this morning. I couldn't raise him.'

'But surely, he could have gone out somewhere—could even be staying somewhere else,' Purdey protested.

'True. Except for one little thing. When I came over here this morning, there was a man in the apartment, he knocked me down and got away, but he left some old clothes in Stannard's room. Add that to the fact that there's no George and I'm worried—that's why I sent for you, Purdey. You have special knowledge.'

Purdey bridled. 'Knowledge of what?'

Steed had the decency to look uncomfortable. 'Well, you and George. I mean, didn't you and he . . . ?'

'Certainly not.' Purdey blushed, then glared as Gambit grinned at her. 'George is a gentleman.'

'What's that got to do with it,' laughed Gambit.

Steed found himself taking Gambit's side—as Purdey might have remarked, he had all the instincts of a male chauvinist pig. 'I agree, that's no criterion, Purdey. If it were—well—all the gentlemen would be extinct.'

Purdey glared. 'George took me to dinner a couple of times—that's all.'

Steed nodded, then Gambit asked, 'This von Claus lecture thing—who's covering it?'

Steed glanced up. 'Could you?'

'I'll handle it.' At the door, he turned. 'By the way, I can bone up on the lecture set-up on the way there but have you any idea who clobbered you?'

Steed smiled wryly. 'A black Mercedes.'

Gambit nodded, then left, closing the door quietly behind him. Steed turned back to Purdey. 'So you can't help then?'

Purdey grinned. 'I don't like everyone to know all my secrets.'

She got up and walked over to a hall cupboard. She opened it and called Steed over. It was empty. He looked at her quizzically.

'So?'

She pointed into the empty cupboard. 'You see—anorak—waders—deep sea lines. All gone. That means he's gone—fishing.'

Steed smiled. 'And you know where?'

'I think so.'

'Meaning?'

'I rang him when he was leaving. He said he was taking a little trip on the Scottish west coast and he'd be based...'

'Based where?'

'I think I'll have to show you.'

Steed grinned. 'What made you think I'd leave you behind anyway, Purdey?'

The guests of the Society were assembling in the green room next to the lecture hall. The Society had made its headquarters in a large country house that they had bought from an impoverished nobleman, and the large car park in front of the house was filling up. Members of the Society and their associates had been looking forward to von Claus's lecture. They had been promised something special and it looked as if the lecture hall would be full for it.

Ralph arrived in good time for the lecture and parked the black Mercedes in a convenient place for a quick exit if necessary. As he crossed the car park he glanced round and saw that the van with the strange soft top was parked where it was easily manoevrable.

He went quickly up the steps and into the main house. There was a security guard on the door and Ralph flashed Stannard's ID card at him. The man nodded and let him in.

Ralph saw at once the man he was looking for. Mr Brown-Fitch was the secretary of the Society and the organisation of days like this taxed him to the limit. He was a prissy little man at the best of times and a great snob into the bargain. His smile, as Ralph approached him, was wiped away as soon as he saw the ID card in his hand. He became just another bloody security man. He wrinkled his nose in distaste and pointed Ralph through into the lecture-room.

Most of the guests were seated by the time Ralph got inside, and he picked himself a seat near the front.

The sounds of conversation died down as Mr Brown-Fitch came into the room. Even so, he stood in front of the assembled company and held up his hands for silence.

'Ladies and gentlemen. I have great pleasure in introducing

our most distinguished guest . . . from Germany . . . Doctor Maybach von Claus.'

The German entered the room to polite applause. He was carrying his notes under his arm and there was something in his hands. As the guests looked at it, they could see that it was a block of ice and that the Doctor was wearing rubber gloves. Inside the ice, as he held it in front of him, was what appeared to be the body of some sort of frog.

The Doctor carefully placed the block of ice on the lecture table, then held up one hand to acknowledge the applause. As soon as it had died down, he smiled at them. 'I should explain that I am von Claus.' He pointed at the block of ice and its strange contents. 'This is Albert, my toad.'

There was laughter from the hall and, when it had died, the Doctor, happy that he had secured their attention, said seriously, 'Of the two of us, Albert is surely the more important.'

The guests settled down. They knew that they were coming to the meat of the lecture and quite early on—an unusual change for such lectures.

Von Claus got quickly to the meat of his subject. He knew he was talking to a Society that was mainly composed of the scientifically minded, and he did not have to make too heavy an introduction to what he wanted to talk about.

'As you know, it is not unheard of for hibernatory animals such as this one—the common toad—to remain naturally in a state of suspended animation for periods amounting even to many years. That is the common toad.'

He paused, then indicated the block of ice. 'But Albert here is a very uncommon toad. Nor is his present, let us say chilly, condition natural. Albert is in fact the hub of a scientifically controlled experiment. I put Albert into his present predicament. Ten years ago, I froze him, but hopefully, not for death. With resuscitation techniques I wish to demonstrate to you now it is my intention to bring Albert back to life again.'

A murmur of disbelief ran round the room, but the Doctor put up his hand.

'I do not mean resurrection, for he has never really died. I will simply bring him back to the land of the living, without any pain and none the worse for his experience.

'We must show a little patience. I already started the melting

33

process before the beginning of the lecture, but it will take a few minutes for the melting to be complete enough for me to be able to remove Albert from his protective covering and go about my business of bringing him back to life.'

'Just what is it you are trying to prove,' asked a voice from the hall.

'I am trying to prove that if you apply the right freezing techniques it is possible to hold a living organism in a state of suspended animation until the right surgical techniques are ready to revive and perform the operation that would renew whatever disease the victim was suffering from. Now, for a long time scientists have known how to do the freezing. The technique that has not been perfected is that of resuscitation. I now believe that I have perfected that technique and that it is Albert here who will prove it to you.'

He turned back to the desk. The ice had almost all melted leaving a pool of water on the wooden desk. In the centre of this was sitting what looked like a very dead toad.

Ralph leaned forward in his seat as the Doctor went to work on the toad with his special instruments. He talked as he did so, but none of the technical jargon he used meant anything to the young man. It was only the result that he was interested in.

After a while the Doctor stepped back. 'Now we must wait a moment.'

Even as he spoke, there came a sudden convulsive movement on the table and the toad moved forward, its eyes blinking open. On the table Albert had suddenly become a very lively toad.

The seated scientists and their friends rose and began to applaud the Doctor, who acknowledged the respect they showed him with smiles and blushes. Only Ralph did not applaud. Instead his gaze went to the window. The van with the soft top was moving closer to the house and that brought a more important smile to his lips. He watched until the van came to a halt, placed so that it could back with no trouble to the side of the house—the windows of the green room. So far everything was going according to plan.

The movement of the van was not the only activity outside. One moment later, Mike Gambit swung his car into the long drive. He knew he was late and he was annoyed with himself for dawdling on the road while he had briefed himself on Doctor von Claus's experiments. The technique of body freezing he knew well—it was much used in open heart operations—so he could not see what was so special here. Still, there had been a tip and that's what Steed's department was for—to follow up tips that could not be handled in the conventional manner.

He pulled into the car park and stopped his car. The first thing he saw was a large black Mercedes and, as he glanced at it, he remembered Steed's crack about his attacker. On an impulse he parked his own car next to the Mercedes, then strode up to the house.

He was met at the door by a security man. 'Can I help you, sir.'

He produced his ID card. 'I'm Mike Gambit.' Then, on another impulse. 'Is Mr George Stannard here?'

'He's inside, sir.'

'How long has he been here?'

'He arrived just before the lecture, sir.'

'Is it still going on?"

'It should just about be over, sir. You'll find everyone in the green room on the right.'

Mike thanked the man and went on up the steps. He was rather looking forward to seeing George Stannard if he was there—or whoever had taken his place if he was not.

Chapter Three

As Gambit ran up the steps into the building, the security man had been inaccurate by a few minutes. The lecture was in fact still underway as von Claus summed up his experiments.

'Already in America the dead are being placed in cold storage against the day when we scientists can awaken them. Men who, a few years ago, would have been pronounced dead, are being kept alive, artificially, indefinitely. Albert here points the way to many miracles, a sleep, a living death if you wish to call it that—and then controlled resuscitation—the awakening from the dead. We have conquered the moon—but if we are to go to the further planets, then we must find the ways and means to send astronauts upon journeys that may have to last a hundred years. I think we are but one step away from achieving that.'

He bowed to show that he had finished and the applause came raining down again. Mr Brown-Fitch was standing by the door as the applause died down and he said, in a high squeaky voice, 'Now, ladies and gentlemen, drinks are being served in the next room, if you would care to move through.'

There was a general exodus towards the door. Von Claus remained on the platform, putting Albert in a special carrying box which he handed to an assistant, then gathered up his papers.

One other man stayed in his place. Ralph leaned forward and watched the Doctor very closely for a while before standing up and moving through into the green room as soon as the Doctor became aware of his presence.

Gambit entered the green room and was quickly provided with a drink—and a speared olive to go with it. A couple of the guests tried to engage him in conversation, but he was only interested in finding Mr Brown-Fitch. He asked one of the people who accosted him to point out the man. He was directed to a small man in the centre of the room, at that moment engaged in conversation with a statuesque blonde.

Mike Gambit went straight over and, with his eyes on the blonde, he asked, 'Mr Brown?'

The girl smiled. 'No, he is.' Then she moved away, but not before her eyes had told Mike that she would like to talk to him—later on.

Brown-Fitch sniffed at the newcomer. He wasn't much of a man but he was enough of one to be annoyed at the newcomer driving the girl away. 'My name is Brown-Fitch, actually. That's Brown-hyphenated-Fitch.'

By way of a reply Gambit produced his ID card and thrust it into the other man's face. 'Mike Gambit. There's no hyphen, I'm afraid. I'm with Steed—I want to ask you something.'

The other man sighed. 'Well, go on.'

Gambit gripped his shoulder hard and propelled him across the room against his will so that they faced one of the windows that overlooked the car park. He sipped his drink then grimaced. 'What is this you're serving?'

Brown-Fitch sniffed again. 'It's schnapps. We're serving it in deference to our lecturer, Doctor von Claus.'

'Well, it's lousy.'

'Schnapps is . . . a very versatile drink.'

Gambit grunted. 'Yes, they used to run their bombers on it during the war. The ones that didn't come back.'

Brown-Fitch sniffed more loudly still. 'Was that your question?'

'No.' He pointed down into the car park. 'That black Merc down there—you got any idea who it belongs to?'

Brown-Fitch reacted with an even louder sniff than before and also by stepping back a pace as if Gambit had suddenly developed a particularly bad smell.

'I'm not a car-park attendant you know.'

Gambit turned on him. Something in his face made Brown-Fitch fear almost for his life. Gambit jabbed him hard in the ribs with one finger as he snapped off his words. 'Which is a great pity, little man. Because he would know. Find out for me will you—there's a good little Brown-Fitch.'

He turned away abruptly and walked across the room towards where the blonde was waiting for him.

At the far end of the room, the object of Gambit's enquiries was sipping his own schnapps with evident pleasure and was looking out of one of the long casement windows that let out on to the car park. They came flush to the floor, but were a few feet up from the ground outside. Slowly, he unlatched the window, so that it would open to the slightest push, but looked closed to anyone glancing casually at it.

Near by, von Claus was conversing in fluent German with one of the other guests. Ralph walked over and joined them, listening to their conversation. When the Doctor finished the conversation, Ralph said, in German, 'Excuse me, Doctor— may I have a word with you?'

Von Claus turned and beamed at him. 'Your German is excellent young man.'

'Thank you, sir.'

'It is just the accent—forgive me, but I can't quite place the district you are from.'

Ralph cut him short with a grin. 'Then perhaps it would be easier to talk English, eh?' He turned and, with a natural movement, he took the Doctor's arm. They began to move towards the opened casement window. 'Doctor, that was a most interesting lecture—but there are one or two points I would take issue on...'

Gambit was looking deep into the blonde's eyes when Brown-Fitch took his revenge. He came over and thrust himself self-importantly between them.

'It's about time your lot got together, wasting the tax-payers money by doubling up all the time.'

Gambit glared at the smirking man as the blonde drifted away.

'Who rattled your cage?'

'A foul-up... not more than one would expect of course...'

'What do you mean?'

'You asked me to check on that black Mercedes. I have found time to check, in spite of all my other duties, and I have found the owner.'

'And?'

'It's one of your own people.'

'Who, man?'

'Stannard.'

Gambit grabbed his arm so hard that the little man winced with pain.

'What do you mean—Stannard?'

As he spoke, Ralph had edged the Doctor right to the window. He glanced out and saw that the van was underway, moving slowly close to the window. He had to wait until it was in exactly the right position. He turned back and said abruptly to the Doctor, who seemed to be losing interest in him,

'But surely, the theory of suspended animation is just that— just a theory.'

Von Claus beamed with the look of a teacher about to address an intelligent but ignorant pupil. 'All scientific conjecture begins as theory.'

'But Doctor...'

As he spoke, he saw that the van was in position. Quickly, he grabbed the Doctor's arm and pushed, falling through the opening window with him. The two men hit the soft top of the van, which opened to admit them, closing quickly after they had fallen through. It was as if they had sunk into quicksand and it was so rapid that no one else in the room noticed what had happened.

The van revved and moved forward from the window, circled the car park to the drive and away.

Brown-Fitch was still too frightened and affronted to be able to speak clearly in answer to Gambit's insistent questions. 'You mean Stannard is here? George Stannard?'

At last he managed to splutter, 'Of course—I checked his ID personally.'

'Well—where is he?'

Brown-Fitch turned and pointed down the room. 'He's over there by the window, talking with Doctor von Cl—'

His voice trailed away. All he and Gambit could see at the far end of the room was an empty space and an open casement window.

Gambit reacted at once and began forcing his way through the guests. He moved so fast that he seemed to slither through them like a snake. Brown-Fitch, following helplessly in his wake caused more trouble as he bounced from guest to guest, spilling their one blessing, the obnoxious schnapps.

Gambit leaned out of the window and saw the van driving away at speed. He almost overbalanced and Brown-Fitch, pushed back by someone he had barged into, came hurtling to the window unable to pull up in time. Gambit hesitated for a fraction of a second, then turned to the little man.

'Brown-hyphen-Fitch—is the Fitch in your name spelt with a small "f" or a big one?'

It seemed hardly relevant but the little man found himself answering almost automatically, 'A big "F".'

Gambit grinned. 'It suits you.'

He leaped from the window before the other man could think up a reply, leaving Brown-Fitch gasping after him.

Gambit let himself go loose as he hit the gravel, rolled over once and came back up on his feet none the worse for the jump. He ran through the parked cars until he reached his own. By now he knew that the van would have reached the road. There was no time to lose. He had no idea why von Claus had been taken by the man impersonating Stannard, but he damned well wanted to find out. All else apart, it might put him one up on Steed—who always got both the bright ideas and the girl.

He started his machine, revved the motor, then backed out of his parking place, sending up a shower of gravel in all directions. He made a turn in a cloud of gravel-dust that made the driveway look as if it had been hit by a sandstorm, then skidded down the drive ruining the paintwork on at least half a dozen cars as he accelerated.

Gambit took the car down the drive in a series of skids and made a drift halt almost sideways at the main gate. He wound down his window and shouted to the attendant, who was pressed up against a tree in mortal danger of his life, 'A van went through here just now—which way?'

The man could only point in the direction that the van had taken. Another shower of gravel and Gambit was away, down the road, gaining by the second on his quarry. They were not going to get away with kidnapping under his very nose if he could help it.

For a while, he saw nothing, then, as he rounded a right-hand bend on the wrong side of the road, he suddenly saw the van ahead of him. As he spotted it, his car went into a four-wheel drift which Gambit corrected with an insolent ease. The van was some quarter of a mile ahead on a straight stretch of road. Gambit put his foot down to close the distance as the van disappeared again round a bend in the road.

Main was driving the van with Gunner in the passenger seat. Ralph was still in the back, looking after their unconscious prisoner. He had fainted from shock when he fell into the van but his unconsciousness was now assisted by the drugs that Ralph had pumped into him.

With van Claus unconscious, Ralph had plenty of time to check up on whether or not they were being followed and, when Gambit's car first skidded into view he shouted out to the others, 'Get a move on. He's after us.'

Now that the van had taken a bend between itself and the car, it made Ralph no less nervous. When the car came into sight again, it was a good deal closer than it had been before. 'He's still with us.'

Main turned from the wheel for a moment. 'How fast is he catching up with us?'

'Too fast.'

'But we have not much farther to go.'

Ralph snarled, 'It is still too far. He will have caught us. He must be stopped. I know what has to be done.'

Main nodded and hefted a Luger into view which he handed to the younger man before saying, 'It was always a possibility, we agreed?'

'It is all right. I am prepared.'

41

Main managed to smile. 'You talk as if you are a dead man. You will rejoin us later, of that I am sure, my friend.'

Ralph was not reassured, but he nodded his thanks to the other man, who, returning the nod, said, 'We will drop you on the next bend.'

The van was approaching another bend as Ralph crawled past his unconscious prisoner and his hand gripped the handle of the rear door. The van turned the corner and Main had one last word for him. 'If you have to die—die bravely.'

Ralph nodded, opened the rear door and leaped out. The van had not slowed to facilitate his exit. He hit the ground and rolled expertly, curled up in a ball so as to do himself the least amount of damage and he came up to a crouching position with his gun steady and at the ready.

The van sped on, the noise receding, as the noise of Gambit's car came closer round the bend. Ralph was in the road crouched and ready, a killing machine primed for its job.

Gambit put his foot right down. Here, he knew the road entered a series of small bends from which a number of sideroads radiated off. It was important that he keep as close behind the van as possible or the chances of him losing it would grow with every bend they took.

He turned the wheel to take the bend, the car going into a slide as it slewed round. Suddenly, in front of him, crouched in the middle of the road, he saw a figure holding a gun up in a two-handed professional grip. There was no adequate avoiding action that Gambit could take with the car. He could only gun the motor even more and pray.

As for Ralph he remained rock steady and firm in the face of the approaching machine as it sped towards him. He raised the gun in both hands and fired once.

Gambit flung himself along the seat as the windscreen was shattered by the first shot. Ralph changed the direction of his aim immediately, firing this time at the front off-side tyre. He found the target, the car lurched, spun out of control, skidded round and climbed a bank at the side of the road where it stopped at a dizzying angle.

Ralph still had his Luger at the ready and he moved towards the car. The only way that he was going to be able to check up on the occupant was to climb up the bank to the upper side of the car. He proceeded to climb up to the upper side, while Gambit, who could hear him coming, crouched down, waiting and hoping that his timing would be right.

Ralph heaved himself up by the side of the car, thus helping Gambit to know exactly where he was and aiding Gambit's timing. As Ralph stretched himself up to look in the side window, Gambit swung the door open as fast as he could and the move was worth the risk. Ralph was hit hard in the stomach. He fell in one direction, his gun went in the other. As Ralph cried out Gambit slid out of the car on the other side and was in time to see Ralph roll down the bank and come back to the crouch position, his eyes flickering around, looking for the gun.

He spotted where it had slid, some way down the road behind him. He half turned to go for it, then turned back and saw Gambit was ready for him. He was standing between Gambit and the gun—that was some comfort to him—but he knew he could not reach the weapon without bringing the other man down on top of him.

Ralph straightened confidently and regarded his opponent. Gambit responded by straightening in his turn. The challenge between them was almost electric and, as they looked at each other across the space, both men became utterly still—save for the darting movements of their eyes. They held this stillness for a long, long time.

Gambit's eyes flicked acknowledgement as Ralph raised his heels slightly—anticipating the action he was going to take. Gambit remained completely motionless and the other man lowered his heels again, though the tension remained in his body.

Both men now held each other's eyes. Two men absolutely still on an English country road—facing each other with the wary stillness of the ancient Samurai of Japan.

It was Ralph who made the first move. He suddenly darted forward with a feinting move. At the last moment, Gambit moved quick and clean. Ralph went past him without being able to touch him with the heel of his flying hand and when they came to a halt the situation was the same—save that it was Gambit who now stood between the other man and his gun.

43

Once more the period of stillness, once more the period of preparation for the attack. Then Ralph could keep the stillness no longer. The other man's complete calm had to a degree unnerved him. He launched a terrific attack and Gambit had only a split second to decide whether to avoid it and wear him down further or to go in for the kill.

He chose the latter. As Ralph arrived at his attack point, Gambit's elbow slammed hard into his chest, half turning the man away and knocking the wind out of his body. As he turned, the elbow went to work and landed a number of heavy blows on his attacker's rib cage.

Ralph was in agony and completely disorientated by the speed and power of Gambit's defensive blows. The latter added the coup-de-grace by bringing the heel of his hand up under Ralph's chin. There was a dull crack as Ralph's teeth closed on his tongue; his eyes rolled up in his head as he slumped forward and hit the ground hard. Gambit jumped out of the way of the falling body. If it had hit him it might have ruffled him.

Gambit bent over the unconscious man and dragged him over to the side of the road, propping him up against the side of his damaged car. He lifted Ralph's eyelid and looked with a frown at the up-turned eyeball underneath. He hoped that he had not hit him too hard. He wanted him conscious for questioning quite quickly or he knew that he would lose the Doctor altogether. Already he was annoyed with himself and the efficiency of Ralph's gun attack, for losing the van. The only way to recover some advantage was in his hands.

He walked back into the road and picked up the Luger pistol. It was a war-time model and Gambit frowned. There were not many of these guns in use now and it was unusual to find one being used for criminal purposes in a quiet English country lane over thirty years after the end of the war.

Ralph was still lying quite still and, with a curse of annoyance at the efficiency of his own strength, Gambit opened the bonnet of his car and located and pulled out the plastic flask that fed the windscreen cleaning sprays. He unscrewed the top and threw the contents into the unconscious man's face.

After a moment, the water did its trick. Ralph spluttered and his eyes fluttered open, focusing on nothing at first, then coming into direct focus on his captor. If looks could have killed, Gambit knew that he was a dead man. He hefted the Luger in his hand to show that he held all the cards and beamed down at his prisoner.

'Welcome back. I am going to ask you some questions now. And you are going to answer them.'

Ralph's accent was thick with panic. 'Why should I?'

Gambit kept his voice quite even. 'You are going to answer them because, when you tried to kill me, you threw away the rule book—understand?'

The man stared at him in silence and Gambit started his questions.

'What is your name?'

'George Stannard.'

Gambit hit him hard on the side of the face. The blow made a sound like a pistol crack in the quietness around them. There was blood on the corner of Ralph's mouth.

'I said what is your name.'

Ralph shook his head. 'I will not tell you anything.'

'Oh, yes you will.'

Ralph stared up at him just one more time, then his mouth started working, a capsule appeared between his teeth and he bit into it. Gambit's reactions to what he was seeing were just a split second too slow. He leaped forward and tried to prise the man's jaws apart. He succeeded only when Ralph suddenly arched up, convulsed and died from the poison he had taken and the empty capsule fell into Gambit's hand.

He let go of the dead man and stared down at the capsule. Poison pills were something out of books or films. He had never seen a man actually kill himself by using one before. Then he reacted as he saw the top of the dead man's head. There was something funny about his hair and Gambit leaned forward to touch it.

The toupee the man was wearing fell away, revealing a shaved pate—like the hairdressing job that was done on monks.

Gambit squatted back on his haunches to think out the events he had witnessed and the bizarre angles he had come up against. Men fanatical enough to kill themselves rather be questioned—men whose heads were shaved like monks. He could only hope that Steed and Purdey were getting somewhere with whatever investigations they were following.

He rose at last and started to walk down the road—to find a phone box and get 'Mother's' specialists out for a clearing-up operation before the dead man and the accident should fall into the hands of the police. That was another rule of the department. Not only was their work to be done as much as possible in secret, but the results were to surface as seldom as possible. It was a rule that Gambit found irritating but necessary. At least, this time, it might get him a lift back to town.

Steed and Purdey had in fact got much further with their investigations by the time Gambit was trying to question the suicide-bent fanatic. They had spent most of the time covering the distance between London and the west coast of Scotland at record speed with the aid of fast cars and an army helicopter.

Now they had arrived in the little coastal town which, according to Purdey, who seemed to know her way around surprisingly well, was what Stannard used as his headquarters when he was on one of his fishing trips.

The car that had been waiting for them at the RAF base some thirty miles away in the Fort William direction now brought them to the waterfront where the gulls were screaming and wheeling over the returned fishing smacks, waiting and hoping for their share of the catch.

There were three inns near the quay and Purdey went unhesitatingly towards one of them. 'He always stays here.'

Steed made no comment but swung his umbrella as he walked along behind her. She opened the door to the entrance to the hotel part of the inn and walked in as if she owned the place.

The landlord was behind the desk in the hall and he looked up with a smile of welcome for an old customer—a smile that turned to a questioning frown as he saw Mr Steed. The look said everything about what the landlord thought of gentlemen escorting to his hotel ladies who had already been brought there by favoured customers.

If she were aware of the implications of the moral judgement being made on her, Purdey gave no sign of it, but smiled her sweetest smile. 'Hello, Mr Barker. How's the fishing?'

46

He grudgingly returned the smile. 'Well enough.'

'Have you seen Mr Stannard this week?'

The landlord glanced again to where Steed stood slightly behind Purdey, his bowler hat at a rakish angle, leaning on his umbrella. Purdey intervened with a word of explanation.

'It's all right, Mr Barker. Mr Steed is Mr Stannard's boss.'

Steed smiled vacuously. 'We seem to have mislaid the dear boy.'

Barker renewed his glare. His worst fears about the effete English were being realised.

'Has he been here?' asked Purdey.

The man nodded reluctantly and Purdey breathed a sigh of relief. So far, so good. 'Is he staying here?'

'Yes, miss.'

'Alone?'

The man shuffled his feet, then. 'Yes, miss.'

Purdey gave her widest, most seductive smile. 'I don't suppose you'd let me have the key to his room—that is, unless he's in. I'd like to give him a surprise.'

The landlord considered this and Purdey added quickly, 'Mr Steed will stay down here with you. He has some questions for you.'

The landlord nodded, reached up, got the key from its hook and handed it to Purdey. She turned to Steed who nodded and she headed for Stannard's room to carry out her search, while Steed leaned across the desk and tried to fix Mr Barker with the male equivalent of Purdey's smile.

'Does Mr Stannard have regular spots in which he fishes?'

Barker hesitated before he nodded. 'Usually, yes.'

'Usually?'

The landlord wondered whether or not to confide, decided at last in favour of frankness. 'Well, he has his usual places but this trip he seemed to be after something different—not so much good fishing, you understand, but a different place to do it. He's been up and down the coast all week.'

'And when was the last time you saw him?'

The landlord frowned as if the question had triggered something off in his mind—something unusual. 'It was the night before last, sir. He was in late in the bar—talking to my barman.'

'What about—do you know?'

The landlord nodded, still frowning. 'I couldn't quite make it out when the man told me. I think he was looking for somewhere to fish where there was a monastery.'

'And he hasn't been seen since?'

'No, sir.'

'Have you told the police?'

'Why should I, sir? Mr Stannard often stayed out for a couple of days when he's fishing—and the deep-sea bass are running well this year. I know he'd fancy landing a few.'

Purdey reappeared and began to approach Steed. He shook his head and pointed the ferrule of his umbrella at the dining-room of the inn. She obeyed at once and disappeared through the door. Steed lifted his bowler to the man he had been questioning.

'I think that luncheon is the next order of the day—you wouldn't have any fish on the menu, would you?'

Steed and Purdey both sat, replete, in the corner of the dining-room where they had eaten. Only when they had finished did Steed, who had ploughed his way through the menu, while Purdey had eaten only the smallest steak and salad, put up a hand and asked, 'Any luck?'

Purdey shook her head. 'I went through George's room with a fine tooth-comb. There's nothing that tells us anything. So it's a wasted journey.'

Steed was indignant. 'Wasted. You should have tried the Coquille St Jacques.'

Purdey laughed. Steed was never rattled. The laughter died as she looked beyond him, out of the window and towards the quay. Steed followed her gaze and saw that a group of people, including the landlord, was gathering down by the quay, staring out at the entrance to the small harbour. Even as they watched, the landlord turned and came hurrying back into the restaurant entrance of the inn. He was out of breath as he came up to their table.

'Mr Stannard must be coming back, sir. His boat's coming into the harbour.'

'His boat?'

'Yes, sir. The one he hired.'

48

Steed and Purdey rose in a flash and left the inn. They hurried down to the edge of the quay and saw what had drawn the crowd to the same spot. The boat was coming slowly into the small harbour, but its occupant seemed to be slumped over the stern, paying no attention to the direction in which he was travelling so slowly. The landlord followed, puffing, in their wake.

'That's him, sir. That's Mr Stannard's boat. Back safe again.'

Steed's voice was tense. 'That boat isn't coming in under power—it's drifting.'

The boat seemed to be making for a deserted point half way down the quay-breakwater and Steed and Purdey hurried forward to the spot. There was a boat-hook lying on the quay and Steed picked it up and reached out. The boat drifted closer and he was able to hook on to the bow and pull it in. Stannard still had his back to them and was taking no interest in the proceedings.

Steed jumped into the boat, balanced himself against the sudden rocking he had set up and moved to pull Stannard by the shoulder. The dead man slumped over and stared sightlessly at the sky.

Steed removed his bowler and glanced back in Purdey's direction, shaking his head. The girl bit back her tears. The landlord came up with her, stared into the boat for a moment, then turned and ran back up the quay.

Steed climbed back on to the quay. 'Damn. He's calling the police.'

He walked back up the quay with Purdey, stopping only to tell one of the assembled fishermen, an old, reliable looking man, to stay with the boat until they arrived.

It was almost dusk before the police and their surgeon had finished with the body of the late George Stannard and had taken him off to Fort William for further forensic examination.

Much to the annoyance of the local Inspector, Steed had insisted on being present as the police went about their preliminary work on the boat and the body of his colleague. Steed's ID card carried too much weight for the police officer to ignore.

He found Purdey pacing up and down in the lounge. The hint

of tears were gone and she was under control again, hard and objective. When he reported what had so far been found, she frowned. 'There wasn't a mark on him? Not a scratch?'

'Just one. Here.' He touched his cheek. 'But that was all.'

She shook her head. 'There must have been something else. A person just doesn't die—not in George's physical condition. Something must have happened to him.'

Steed was staring out of the window, a frown of concentration on his face.

'Well, we'll know more when the forensic report is in. They should have it for us by tomorrow—can I borrow your lipstick?'

Purdey nodded absently and opened her bag. It was only as she handed it to him, that she reacted to the strange request. 'Lipstick?'

Steed turned away from her, opened the cylinder and made a vertical mark on the window pane. He was diverted for a moment by the colour.

'What a pretty shade of pink.'

Purdey reacted automatically with a snort. 'Pink? It's called The Sins of Youth.'

'That's not a colour. That's an accusation.' As he spoke he added a horizontal line, making a cross on the pane, peering through it.

'Exactly what are you doing?' asked Purdey.

'I'm trying to get a fix. Yes, I'd say that the boat drifted in roughly from the north-west—now what lies north-west of here.'

Purdey could not restrain a chuckle. 'America.'

Steed turned and gave her a baleful look. 'Besides America?'

She shrugged. 'I don't know.'

Steed renewed his frown at her ignorance. 'I know there are some islands out there—but which one would lie directly north-west?'

It was the landlord who provided the answer. He came in at that moment carrying a tea tray, laden with all sorts of scones and jams as well as the tea and cups. It looked more like a full meal than the tea that is usually served in London, and Steed's eyes lit up. The landlord said, 'That'd be the Isle of St Dorca.'

'St Dorca? What happens there?' asked Purdey.

'It used to be mainly a fishing place—until the war that is—

50

since then, well, it's mainly the brothers that run it, a sort of retreat.'

Steed frowned. 'Retreat? Brothers?'

'The Brothers of St Dorca. It's a Holy Order. Monks.' As he spoke, he glanced out of the window. 'There's some of them coming down to the quay now, sir. On their way back to the island.'

Steed went to the window in time to see monks in brown habits loading boxes and a large hamper on to a motor-boat.

The landlord went on, 'They come ashore once in a while to buy provisions—and to sell their extract.'

'Extract?'

'St Dorca Fish Extract, sir. It's a kind of preservative.'

Purdey joined Steed at the window. The loading was completed; the boat had been pushed off from the quay and was making for the mouth of the harbour. They watched as it reached the open water, then set off in a north-westerly direction. Steed squinted along the cross he had made. It would seem that he had been right in his estimate of the direction from which Stannard's boat had come. He did not know what it all added up to—but he was determined to find out.

It was Main and Gunner who had supervised the loading of the supplies and hamper. After they had got away from Gambit, they had gone to the hiding place of their helicopter—an old air-field abandoned since the war, and had made the flight up to Scotland, landing again in a deserted glen where the familiar truck that the brothers used for their business on the mainland was waiting for them.

During the flight Doctor von Claus had regained conscious-ness and they had quieted him again with a sedative so that he was sleeping peacefully when they arrived. They had carried him to the lorry where a large hamper was waiting for his further transportation and had put him inside.

There were other items already piled in the lorry to make their departure from the mainland look even more convincing and they had quickly reached the harbour and the boat, unaware that they were being observed.

It was only when they were well out at sea, that Main glanced down at the hamper and saw that the end of von Claus's tie was sticking out. It had been lucky that there was no one close when they had loaded the boat up.

Steed got up from his tea and told Purdey that they would be going back to London that night. In the meantime, he telephoned his service in London to see if there were any messages from Gambit on the lecture, or how it had gone. There was a message right enough: The Doctor had been kidnapped, there had been a chase and a death. Michael Gambit was still explaining it all away to the police.

Steed came back and joined Purdey, telling her briefly what had happened. She asked, 'Do we stay here and investigate?'

He shook his head. 'No, we go back, Mike might have got something more concrete to go on.'

He was at the door, bowler hat on, umbrella at the ready before she had time to get up.

Chapter Four

The journey back to London had taken most of the night and Purdey retired to her own flat promising to meet Steed at his house at eleven the next morning. When she arrived for the meeting some fifteen minutes late, as is a woman's privilege even in these liberated days, Gambit still hadn't arrived.

Steed answered the door to her and led her through to the study. It was a very masculine room in both concept and colour. It was furnished and decorated with superbly elegant pieces that Steed had collected down the years, many of them in sharp contrast to one another, so that modern toy soldiers rubbed shoulders with Chippendale chairs, Ming vases with English shot-guns. On a side table were silver-framed photographs of some of Steed's old co-workers: Cathy Gale, Emma Peel and Tara King. Purdey knew better than to ask Steed about them.

Without a word, Steed handed Purdey a document he had received earlier that morning—the official autopsy report on the late George Stannard. As she settled down on the edge of the desk to study it, he walked across the room to where a violin case lay open on a chair and picked up the violin and bow from within.

He put the violin in the playing position under his chin and began to saw away, making a noise that made Purdey wince with an almost physical pain—Steed had never been particularly musical.

In spite of the noise he was making she managed to finish the report, then looked up in surprise. 'Boiled down, this says that George died of fish poisoning.'

Steed nodded without interrupting the cacophony he was creating. 'That's right—poor old George died of fish poisoning—the only question is—How?'

Purdey shrugged. 'An oyster too many?—or perhaps a herring bit him?—do you have to keep on doing that?'

Steed stopped abruptly. 'Well, it was supposed to help Sherlock Holmes when he was trying to work something out—and let's face it, we need all the help we can get at the moment.'

Purdey held up the report. 'Besides this, what do we have at the moment?'

'George is dead—von Clous has disappeared, kidnapped—the whole thing's a dead end.'

'Very dead,' said Gambit from the doorway.

Steed put down the violin. Gambit was holding the Luger that he had taken from Ralph, in a plastic bag.

'Well, what do you have, then?'

Gambit put the gun on the desk. 'Our German friends were very co-operative and efficient as usual—but it doesn't help us very much.'

'What did they give you?'

'Well, this Luger was issued to one Oberführer Fritz Gunner in December of 1942.'

'Do we know where he is now?'

'He's missing, presumed dead.'

Steed swore under his breath. 'How and when?'

'It appears that Fritz Gunner was on DER ADLER FLIGHT K7—one of the last planes to leave Berlin in 1945—just before the Russians overran the city. Neither he nor the plane has been seen since.'

Steed sighed and gave a look of regret and apology to Purdey before he picked up the violin again. 'Oh, I'm afraid it's back to the old fiddle.'

Before he was able to make the first excruciating noise,

Gambit interrupted him. 'There is a link, Steed—a German gun—von Claus.'

'I know, but a link to what and where?'

Gambit pulled a report from his pocket, similar to the one that Purdey was still holding. 'The autopsy on the man who killed himself in front of me makes fun reading, too. Apparently he died of fish poisoning.'

Purdey snapped, 'So did Stannard.'

Steed snatched the report from Gambit. 'Is there anything about what sort of fish poisoning?'

'Probably a concentrated extract from the poison sac of the jelly fish or a similar creature.'

Purdey almost shouted in her excitement, 'An extract—Steed.'

Steed spoke softly, as if it were all coming to him at the same moment. 'The Monks of St Dorca specialize in fish extract.'

It was Gambit's turn to be surprised. 'Monks. Did you say monks?'

'What about it?'

For reply, Gambit took something from his pocket. It was another clear plastic envelope and inside was what looked like a toupee. He let it fall on the desk. 'Take a look at this.'

'So?'

'The man who died was wearing this.'

'So, he was vain.'

'But don't you see. His head was shaved in the middle like a monk's and he wore this to cover it.'

'I stand corrected. It seems we do have a lead to our problem. Whatever is going on, the answer seems to lie on the Island of St. Dorca.'

'We'd better get up there again,' said Purdey impatiently.

Steed shook his head. 'I don't think it'll be quite as simple as that. We'll have to make our approaches in different ways. Sit down and we'll work out our strategy.'

On the Island of St Dorca, the objects of Steed's attentions were going about their business much as usual. The fishermen in the village were mending their nets and the monks were doing their normal work in the monastery. The only major difference in routine was in the office of the Abbot where Father Trasker was sitting behind his desk, looking at his pale, disheveled visitor and wringing his hands in apology as he stared at a frightened von Claus.

'Doctor von Claus, what can I say to you—I owe you—I offer you—the deepest and most humble apologies.'

Seeing that the man opposite him seemed to be in such distress, von Claus's feelings turned from fear and bewilderment into something approaching anger as the other man went on, 'Had I had the slightest suspicion that the young men of this island planned such a prank—utterly iniquitous— unforgivable—the only saving grace is that they apparently meant well.'

Von Claus half-rose, felt his legs, still weak from the drugs, giving under him and sat down again before snapping angrily, 'They meant well? I have been kidnapped—drugged.'

Trasker held up his hands in a deprecatory gesture of reassurance, as if this would be enough to draw the anger from the other man.

'Yes, yes, I agree—but their motives for such an act, I can assure you that they were above reproach. Please, Doctor, calm down and take some tea with me, so that I may explain.'

Von Claus went quite purple in the face, anger finally removing the last traces of pallor from his face. 'Take tea? While half the country is looking for me. I want a telephone, that is all.'

Trasker gave a beatific smile. 'Unfortunately we have no telephone link with the mainland—but I have arranged for a boat to be made ready for your return.'

'How soon, that is all I want to know?'

'Very soon, Doctor. In the meantime, I would welcome the opportunity of explaining what has happened.'

As he spoke he lifted a little bell and rang it once. A monk entered immediately and Trasker said, 'We will take tea, brother.'

Father Trasker turned his attention back to the angry man in front of him. 'Doctor von Claus, a few weeks ago, one of our most revered brothers fell into a coma. Since then, all efforts to revive him have failed.'

Von Claus frowned. 'But surely there are doctors here?'

'Yes, indeed—and some of the monks here are skilled in medical matters—nor do we lack equipment—but we do lack your brilliance.'

As he said these last words he fixed his light blue eyes on the Doctor and the man shrank back slightly as he saw the intensity that was unveiled in them for a second—a complete contrast with the conciliatory manner and speech of the man. A second later the eyes were veiled again—a middle-aged man out of his depth in an embarrassing situation, but von Claus had seen enough to allow fear to return to him. Trasker went on.

'You must understand—the man in a coma is much loved—regarded by some as a saint—that is why our more headstrong young men took such desperate measures.'

The Doctor said cautiously, 'Why didn't they just come to see me and ask me?'

'Would you have come?'

The two men regarded each other for a moment and von Claus had to admit the justice of the question. Father Trasker said gently, 'You must receive many pleas for assistance—more than you could possibly deal with.'

He faded into silence, seeing a frown of concentration crossing von Claus's brow as the kidnapped man debated the extent to which it was wise to co-operate. At last he asked, 'A boat is being made ready for me, you say?'

'Yes, Doctor.'

'Well, while I am waiting, I might as well take a look at this man. It can do no harm.'

Father Trasker rose and helped the Doctor out of his chair. 'I cannot begin to thank you.'

'Don't thank me, yet. There may be nothing I can do.'

The man in the coma was lying in one of the cells that were occupied by the monks. The unconscious man was Father McKay and he was lying in a coffin-like container on top of a medical trolley. He was clothed in a special thermal suit—his face swaddled with medical cloths, while around his body in the container the space was packed with ice—lines and tubes led from the container and the man to various pieces of equipment, some of it for refrigeration, some of it for a life-support system.

Sitting, watching the equipment, was Karl, the old monk who had led the questioning of George Stannard. There was no hatred in his face now, only anxiety. He was wearing a white habit like a medical orderly in a hospital.

As the cell door opened and Trasker ushered the Doctor in, Karl rose. Father Trasker said, 'This is Brother Bury.'

'Doctor von Claus.'

The Doctor looked past the man's shoulder at the elaborate arrangements that had been put into effect to keep the sick man alive and Father Trasker went on, 'Brother Bury heads our medical team.'

Von Claus inclined his head. 'You've done very well indeed. The freezing techniques seem to have been nicely judged.'

'Thank you, Doctor. Would it be too optimistic of me to say that I would enjoy working with you.'

Von Claus frowned as he considered an answer, then putting the medical considerations ahead of his own rather bizarre position, he nodded. 'We'll need special hyper-thermal equipment—desensitisers.'

'I have anticipated the need for that. The necessary equipment is on its way and should be here at any time.'

Von Claus subjected the other man to a long, penetrating, but professionally not unfriendly stare. 'I will enjoy working with you. Where can I scrub up?'

The rest of that morning was spent in making preparations for the Doctor to carry out his speciality. He had become so immersed in the problems of surgery that confronted him that he put right out of his mind the mysterious way that he had been brought to the island and the monastery and concerned himself only with the medical problems that lay ahead. He was looking forward to working with Brother Bury. The man might only be a medical orderly, but he had learned a lot about medicine at some time in his life—pretty advanced medicine at that. There had been the slight undercurrent of an accent in his British speech and the Doctor suspected that he might be originally German— or at any rate central European in origin.

At last the hyper-thermal equipment arrived and was prepared for use. Only the Doctor and Karl would be in the cell during the operation. With all the equipment that was in use there was no room for any of the others, though Father Trasker was obviously disappointed to be left outside.

Before the operation began, Doctor von Claus explained to his new colleague exactly what he would be doing. 'I have my equipment and the correct materials. I will be making an injection directly into the heart.'

'How big?'

'That is the major question. You will just have to trust my judgement when we do the operation. If he responds in the correct manner, then we will have to bring his temperature gradually up to normal, but working as quickly as possible under the circumstances—you realise of course that this moment in the operation is the one that will open the door either to failure or success.'

Karl nodded grimly. 'I understand, Doctor.'

'Good, then we are ready to begin.'

The two men scrubbed up and were dressed in surgical equipment for the operation. With a corner of his mind the Doctor noticed with admiration that every medical requirement was met immediately. The monastery seemed to be better equipped than most hospitals.

They went alone into the room, leaving Father Trasker and some of the other monks waiting anxiously in the corridor. Doctor von Claus went quickly through the preliminaries on the patient, then the hypodermic was made ready and the crucial part of the operation began.

'I now wish to make the injection into the man's heart.'

The Doctor's voice was muffled by his surgical mask and Karl nodded from behind his, baring the patient's chest to show an indelible mark, placed earlier by von Claus to show the best point of entry to the chest for the heart muscles.

Von Claus came forward and carefully inserted the hypodermic. After what seemed like an infinity of time, he started to depress the plunger. The hypodermic was about half-empty when he stopped and withdrew it. He turned to Karl. 'Now is the moment, the body must respond satisfactorily and we will slowly bring the temperature up to normal—gradually, as I said, but as quickly as possible.'

The two men waited as they fiddled with the dials and controls on the refrigeration machines, slowly raising the temperature of the insulation that surrounded the body, between times, inspecting it for signs of life. They took the temperature up as high as the Doctor indicated that they dared go, then watched carefully. Father McKay was still lying as still as death. For a moment, it seemed to Karl that the operation had done nothing towards restoring him to normal life.

Then, as he watched, the man's chest started to move, spasmodically at first, with hardly any traceable movement. Von Claus almost yelled his elation, 'Oxygen.'

Karl handed him the mask and prepared to work the controls at the head of the cylinder. Von Claus put the mask over the man's face and signalled for Karl to start pumping the oxygen slowly to him. At the same time, he took the man's arm and felt the pulse near the elbow. He called out, 'The pulse beat is strengthening.'

Karl shouted, 'You've done it, Doctor.'

'Yes. You may tell the others.'

Leaving the Doctor to make the final checks on the equipment for the next stage of Father McKays' return to the world, Karl moved to the door and opened it. Father Trasker was waiting outside, almost as if he had been rooted to the spot for the whole period of the operation—which had taken well over three hours.

'Father Trasker, he's done it.'

Von Claus bowed. 'We have done it.'

Karl acknowledged the Doctor's compliment with a return bow. Von Claus was sure that if the man had not controlled himself he might also have clicked his heels. Karl went on, 'You cut corners, Doctor—you take immense, brilliant risks—risks I would never dare to take. You have brought this man back from the dead—I think you are the only doctor in the world who could have done it.'

Father Trasker moved into the cell with the other two men. He saw the man living and breathing in his coffin-like bed and was profoundly moved. Words failed him as he looked down. There were tears in his eyes as he convulsively gripped Dr von Claus's hand. 'Doctor . . .'

Von Claus smiled wearily, running a hand over his forehead and the old Abbot was at once solicitous. 'But you seem as if you are weary—desperately tired. Doctor, your boat is ready, but I must insist that you wait a while before you attempt the trip back to the mainland.'

Reluctantly, von Claus nodded. He desperately wanted to get back to the mainland but realised the truth of Father Trasker's words. At the same time he wanted to see the patient again later, see what progress the man had made. The technique was still only experimental—this was the first man he had tried it on.

'Yes. Yes, I think you are right.'

He began to move out of the cell, then turned abruptly back to Karl. 'The pacemaker—if there is a power failure—if it should fail now . . .' He left the rest of the sentence unfinished, but Karl said steadily, 'Don't worry, Doctor. I shall remain on watch with him. Go on, rest, you deserve it.'

Von Claus once more acknowledged the compliment and left the room with Father Trasker. Karl watched them walk the length of the corridor, then stepped back into the little cell, closing the wooden door carefully behind him. He turned to look down at the breathing, living body of Father McKay, then at the pulse beat on the pacemaker.

As he watched, the smile left his face, to be replaced by a look of total contempt that embraced the Doctor as well as the patient he had revived. He moved over to the switch on the pacemaker and turned it off. The screen went dead at once.

He turned to watch McKay. The unconscious man breathed twice convulsively, then his chest was still—he was dead forever this time. Karl nodded to himself with satisfaction. There would be plenty of time to set the scene for the Doctor to carry out the real operation late that night. Arousing the man from sleep would make his mind slightly disorientated—perhaps he would not even notice the substitution of patient at all until the operation was performed.

The monastery was not the only place buzzing with activity that day. Steed, after his morning conference, had sent Gambit off to Germany on a little research idea attached to the identity of the man who had originally owned the Luger that had been

61

found on Ralph, while he and Purdey made their way to Scotland, each based on an independent mission.

It was thus that, during the operation, the alarm bell pealed from the village, a warning that visitors had arrived. It was Main who had hurried down to the village to see what was going on. There, a surprising sight met his eyes.

A man had arrived at the quay in a small boat. He was dressed as if on his way to the City of London for a business conference, even down to the bowler hat on his head and the furled umbrella on his arm. He was now busy putting ashore his luggage—and from the amount and variety of it, he was planning on a long stay.

Arranging a tight smile on his face, Main strolled down to the quay to greet this eccentric newcomer who was now unloading hampers, a crate of champagne—and, of all things, a billiard cue.

Main said as jovially as he could, 'Good morning.'

Steed looked up from his work with a bright smile. 'And good morning to you.'

Main glanced at all the luggage. 'Are you planning a long stay?'

'No. Maybe a day or two—just a few of life's essentials. A fellow doesn't like to rough it.'

'We'll give you a hand.'

'Thanks.'

Main jerked his head and a number of the fishermen moved towards the piles of luggage, including Gunner, who had been standing near by and who had first rung the warning bell. As Gunner moved past him and went to pick up one of the largest pieces, Main said, sotto voce, 'And search every inch of it.'

When, later, they were able to search all the luggage between them, as Steed went for a convenient and quite deliberate walk through the village, they found nothing but the possessions of a vacuous and selfish traveller.

As they left the room, Main said, 'He's clean.'

Gunner scowled. 'Yes, but why is he here—and who is he?'

The really important link in Steed's plan had arrived on the south side of the island just as he was taking care of all the attention at the quay. Purdey's arrival was a little less comfortable than that of her boss. She emerged from the water like the best-looking submarine in the world, dressed from head to foot in a skin-tight wet suit and a snorkel helmet that had taken care of her underwater breathing problems. She had not swum the whole way from the mainland. Steed had been gentleman enough to give her a lift most of the way.

She walked up the beach, taking off the helmet and shaking out her blonde hair as she looked from left to right to make sure that she was unobserved.

In the distance she heard the peal of bells that told her Steed was doing his stuff in the village. The amount of luggage he had with him would keep them talking for weeks.

As she went up the beach she left a fine set of webbed footprints. She was amused at what the locals might think of those is they spotted them before the tide came in.

It was an uncomfortably short time later that one of the men from the monastery saw the footprints. He held the fishing rod that he carried with him tighter than ever as he ran off to find a companion to tell him that he suspected someone had landed on the island surreptitiously.

She still wore the flippers as she walked on to the headland, then dodged down into cover on one side. Ahead of her was a small cottage and a man sitting on a wall beside it with his back to her. She retreated into cover to remove the flippers and replace them with soft ballet shoes from inside her wet suit.

She was still making the change when she heard voices. Hardy, the young man who had seen the flipper marks had indeed found a fellow security guard. She peered through the trees. They stood in the open beyond, both of them, for some reason—it could hardly be cover—were carrying fishing rods. The other man was speaking.

'What do you mean, frogmen. You must be mistaken.'

'But I saw the marks in the sand, I tell you. They were flipper marks, like a frogman wears.'

'Well, I suppose we'd better take a look around anyway.'

Hardy pointed towards the cottage where the man sat with his back to both them and Purdey. 'What about O'Hara—we could ask him if he's seen anyone?'

'That feeble-minded old fool. If he had seen anything—he'd have forgotten it by now.'

They moved on, turning past the small outcropping of trees to make for the beach. As for Purdey, she retraced her steps a little way to make sure they had really gone, then turned her attention back to the lone man who was sitting so still on his wall, staring out at the Atlantic Ocean.

Steed was still acting out his part as the eccentric sitting target. He was busy forcing his cover on the barman at the local inn where his luggage had finally been put and searched to his satisfaction as well as to that of the men who had searched it.

The grizzled barman was accompanied by a pretty barmaid who had volunteered that her name was Molly. That had given Steed the opening he needed. 'My name's Steed, John Steed. I'm with the Ministry. Culture you know, that sort of thing.'

Molly frowned and lowered her pleasingly plump arms on to the bar so that she billowed out curvaceously from the top of her sweater as an added distraction for the man she had been told to question. 'What exactly do you do, Mr Steed?'

She was the perfect straightwoman for his act and he was pleased to note out of the corner of his eye that everyone else in the bar was paying attention to the answer he was about to give, no matter what they pretended to be doing. He cleared his throat to get the pitch exactly right, not so loud as to be obvious, but loud enough to be distinctly heard by everybody at the bar.

'I go round to look at old ruins—old buildings. Make recommendations for preservation orders—maintain our national heritage and all that sort of thing, etcetera, etcetera—I say, this is jolly good brandy.'

'Another, sir?'

'Certainly.'

As the brandy was handed to him, he noticed out of the corner of his eye that Main had entered the bar and he said loudly, 'Yes, m'dear. I've been sent here to ferret round the place a bit.'

He watched with satisfaction as the otherwise expressionless face of the newcomer tightened slightly round the muscles of the jaw before he turned and left the bar. He turned back to Molly and smiled. 'That's the chap who helped with my luggage. Strange fellow. Didn't take anything for it and now won't stop for a drink.'

Purdey made her cautious way to the cottage, keeping her eyes all the time on the old man on the wall and noticing that he did not turn or stare, even when she was close to him. He was about sixty years old and, between moments of complete stillness, he was casting a small fishing rod, so that the hook hit a tin can some distance away with every cast. Purdey slid on to the wall and sat down beside him as if it were the most natural thing in the world.

'Hello.'

The old man glanced at her, favouring her with a beatific smile. If he were surprised by her wet suit, he gave no sign of it. She was just a pleasant friend visiting an old man.

'Hello, my dear.'

'You're Mister O'Hara, aren't you.'

'Am I?'

She smiled. 'So I'm told.'

He smiled back at her, his eyes gentle. This was no fool, just an old man who forgot what he chose to forget, things were less trouble that way.

'It's the mister that had me fooled for a moment. No one has called me mister in a long while. They all laugh at me—they say that I'm always forgetting things.'

'Doesn't everyone?'

'You forget things too, do you, dear?' His voice was pathetically eager as he asked the question.

'Sometimes.'

He frowned. 'Damn. I forgot what we were talking about.' Then he started laughing, a pleasant sound in the afternoon warmth.

'We were talking about forgetting things.'

'Ah, yes, so we were. I nearly forgot. I don't always forget things though. There's some things that they'd like me to forget.' He said it with such force that Purdey knew she was on to something.

She asked casually, 'What kind of things?'

'Eh?'

'What would they like you to forget?'

'Oh, yes—well, for one thing, they'd like me to forget about the big bird.'

'What big bird?'

It was the old man's turn to be puzzled, but she was beginning to get the hang of the pattern of his conversation. 'Big bird? What big bird?'

'The one you were telling me about.'

'Oh, was I? Oh, that one. Yes. It came swinging out of the sky it did—just like a chariot—you know, the one they're always singing about—bathed in fire it was—a visitation...'

'When was this?'

'When was what?'

'The big bird.'

'Bird?' The old man made another casual cast and hit the tin can as accurately as he had done before. He was only obtuse when he wanted to be, it appeared.

'The bird that fell from the sky,' said Purdey patiently.

'Oh, so you saw it too, did you.'

Purdey seized on the opening. 'Yes, but I can't quite remember when.'

The old man laughed his pleasant laugh again. 'Forgotten, have you? Now that's a bad habit. Why, it was during the war, my dear. A big war. It was between someone... and someone else. It was then the big bird came—but they buried it—buried it deep.'

'Do you know where?' snapped Purdey.

The old man was affronted by the questioning. 'Of course I do. I could take you there this very minute.'

'Really?'

'If I can remember where.'

Purdey jumped down from the wall and held a hand out for him to follow. She gave him her brightest smile. 'Why don't we try?'

'All right, my dear. We will.' He was chuckling as he got down off the wall and beckoned her to follow.

They went round the side of the hut away from the sea and moved up a hill. There was a copse half way up the slope and the old man pointed towards it. She was forced to follow him across the open ground between the cottage and the copse and she kept looking round to make sure that she was not being observed. She was relieved when they at last reached the cover of the copse. He led her through it to a clearing where only small saplings grew. The old man turned to her, a smile of triumph lighting up his face.

'If I remember rightly, it was buried about here.'

Purdey smiled wearily. 'If you remember rightly...' She followed his example and dropped to her knees. As he began to pull and dig at the soil, she followed suit.

He muttered, 'They didn't have time to bury it deep—I do remember that. Mind you, it's empty now. The big bird, they emptied its belly...Some say it was filled with treasure—the greatest treasure in the world...but they took the treasure away.'

Purdey had felt something under the soil and began to clear it with her hands. It was something smooth and metallic—perhaps it really was the fuselage of a crash-landed aeroplane. She saw that there was something on the metal she had uncovered and she scrabbled away at the loose soil to reveal the familiar Nazi cross.

She renewed her efforts and uncovered the piece of fuselage next to the cross. Written on it was the small legend 'DER ADLER K7'.

Next to it was the small German eagle that marked it as an aeroplane of one of the elite. Purdey sat back on her heels and tried to work out what it all meant. Whatever it revealed, she knew now that George Stannard had died for something important and the answer to it was on this island. After all, the Luger that Gambit had taken off the dead man had originally been issued to a man who had last been seen when the DER ADLER K7 had taken off from Berlin in the last days of the war. She wondered what Mike Gambit was finding out on his mission of research in Germany.

She would have been annoyed if she had been able to see him at that moment. Put Mike Gambit in some Government department and he would come up with the prettiest girl working there. The German records office was no exception and at that moment he was leaning over a desk plying his art on Gerda, the prettiest girl in the office, and also the only one who had fully studied the records concerning the disposition of Luftwaffe planes at the end of the war. He was just asking her if they still kept in the archives the records of all flights. She bridled at the questioning of her efficiency, but the annoyance was less than it would have been with a less charming man.

'Of course, Mr Gambit. All flight records are effectively recorded. Which flight in particular do you have in mind?'

'DER ADLER FLIGHT K7.'

'April 1945?'

He was nonplussed by the speed of the answer and his mouth fell open. 'Why, yes...'

The girl smiled.

'I don't have to look for the file on that one.'

'You don't?' He sounded a little disappointed, as if he wanted to stay in her company for longer than she was going to let him.

'It is a famous flight. I know it all by heart. DER ADLER FLIGHT K7 out of Berlin at 22.30 hours on April 29th 1945— are you by any chance from German stock, Mr Gambit?'

'What?'

'It is just that you are very attractive. There is surely some German in you somewhere?'

Gambit shook his head with some regret. 'Sorry...'

'Never mind, I like Englishmen too and I am free for dinner tonight and—'

At any other time, Gambit would have been more than eager to follow up the invitation—but this wasn't any other time. Instead, he interjected hurriedly, 'Where was it heading—Flight K7?'

'South America—it is the curve of your jawline—the square set of your shoulders that...'

'South America?'

The girl pulled herself together, a lovely experience to watch. Her voice was haughty with rejection. 'Mr Gambit, this was the last recorded flight out of Berlin before the surrender—where else could it have been heading?' She softened. 'Your eyes too, they have that distinctly Bavarian...'

He grinned. 'Listen, I think that you are lovely too, but I've got other things on my mind—who was on board the plane?'

She shrugged. The flight was obviously of little interest to her.

'Probably no one save for the essential crew—and the greatest treasure in Germany. At least, that was the rumour.'

'All the gold and art treasures...'

'It is just a rumour Mr Gambit. Unconfirmed.'

'What happened to Flight K7?'

She beckoned him to follow her. On the wall was an air-route map of the Atlantic, Europe and the Eastern seaboard of the United States, criss-crossed with lines and notations of airline and military flight paths. She pointed vaguely at the Atlantic Ocean to the west of Scotland.

'The last radio message pinpointed it as here—mid-Atlantic and still heading west. Presumably the plane was shot down—as you can see, there's nothing here. She lies now at the bottom of the ocean.'

He looked hard at the map and was aware that the girl was still looking hard at him. 'You are quite sure you have no German blood?'

Gambit laughed. 'Oh, I have that.'

'I knew it.'

Gambit glared at her. 'I took three bullets when I was getting across the bloody wall last year. Your people had to give me four transfusions.' She was taken aback by his answer and he grinned. 'Dinner tonight is out of the question. I have to get back to England—but Saturday, perhaps?'

She was almost the caricature of the militarist German. 'I will await your call.'

As he went she called after him, 'Where were you hit?'

'Nowhere that need concern you.'

He went on a couple of paces, then turned and came back to her, she preened herself, but he went past her and stared at the map again.

'You're wrong, you know.'

'Wrong?'

'To say that there's nothing there. There is—a tiny island—the Island of St Dorca.'

He turned and strode from the records office, leaving Gerda

open-mouthed. He glanced at his watch. The flight that was standing by for him could get him to Prestwick by evening—then overland to the mainland facing St Dorca would take till midnight. He had to reach Steed immediately and tell him of his suspicions.

Chapter Five

Purdey stayed in the copse with the uncovered section of the buried German plane until well after dark. O'Hara stayed with her, prattling on, mainly about his inability ever to remember anything, and no more questioning could get any further coherent information out of him.

When darkness came, she suggested to him that he could go back to his cottage—if he could remember where it was—while she herself prepared to descend on the village. She had to talk to Steed about her discovery.

She was right to approach the village with caution. By doing so, she was able to spot the men who might have caught her. Main and Gunner were both hidden in the shadows around the quay, both carrying their fishing rods—a piece of equipment for which she had not worked out the reason—and both of them were bracketing the inn so that if anyone left, they would be able to follow.

Purdey was able to make it across the open space to the inn when their backs were turned and skirt round to the rear. One light was on in the upstairs room and she began to shin cautiously up a convenient drainpipe towards it. Steed had promised to spend the evening in his room if she needed to report to him.

The tiny room was crammed almost to bursting with Steed's luggage. He just had the small area between the bed and the window to move about in, plus a passageway to the door. While Purdey climbed, he was engaged in some contacting of his own. Gambit had arrived at Prestwick and had used a special high frequency to get in touch with him. Steed was at his transmitter-receiver at the moment. For reasons of security—especially if he knew his luggage was going to be searched—Steed carried a special reception set built into a bowler hat. Now it lay on the bed in front of him—he had worn it all day—the aerial poking out of the crown—and he leaned forward to talk into it. He waited for Gambit's reply and listened hard to discern the words through the heavy wall of static:

'...It was rumoured to contain Germany's greatest treasure—and the whole lot must have come crashing down on your island. What would you do if it happened to you?'

Steed considered, then talked into the hat. 'Difficult question. Hypothetical of course. I'm as honest as the day is long.'

'You'd kill off any survivors and pocket the lot. That's what the people of St Dorca seem to have done. And somehow, poor old Stannard must have stumbled on to it and...'

'I can make the equation. Thing is now to prove it.'

He kept to himself a reminder of the von Claus connection. There seemed no way to link his disappearance in with such a theory but there was no point in debating it with Gambit over the short-wave.

He glanced up from his hat as the window opened and Purdey leaned into the room, still perched on the drainpipe outside. 'I wouldn't let too many people see you doing that, Steed. They might think you were talking through your hat.'

Gambit's muffled voice came out of the bowler, 'Is that Purdey? What's she doing?'

Steed answered airily, 'Oh, just hanging around. We'll be in touch, Gambit—over and out.'

In spite of a shout of protest from the bowler, Steed snapped off the switch inside, then lowered the aerial so that it looked like an ordinary bowler hat once more. He looked up at Purdey still perched outside the window.

'Well, what have you found?'

'I found an aeroplane—DER ADLER K7—and I know what it's all about now.'

'Germany's greatest treasure?'

'Yes—how did you know?'

'That's Gambit's theory too.'

Purdey was indignant. 'Theory indeed. There's no other explanation.'

'Perhaps. It's all right as far as it goes, but unfortunately that's not far enough. It still doesn't explain why they snatched von Claus.'

Purdey scrabbled at the sill, then went back to hanging on to the drainpipe. 'Look, if we're having a conference, would you mind giving me a hand to get in?'

'You can't do that. To enter a gentleman's bedroom unchaperoned—very, very dangerous. Not like you at all. What is the world coming to?'

'But you're no gentleman.'

'And that is where the danger lies—goodnight Purdey—you're doing a grand job.'

With that, he closed the window on her, leaving her mouthing volubly outside. He watched her for a moment with quiet amusement, then opened the window once more.

'And another thing...'

Steed held up his hand, cutting her off in mid-flow. 'We must find von Claus.'

He closed the window again and she stared at him in silence this time through the glass. Then she dropped out of sight as she began to climb back down to the ground.

From the shadows, Main watched her descent. He had heard the muffled voices as she and Steed had spoken and had taken up a watching position at the side of the building. Now, sensing that he would learn about the mission by stealth rather than the frontal attack of catching her at once, he began to follow her as she made her cautious way through the sleeping village in the direction of the monastery.

Purdey was not aware that she was being followed. Her mind was turning over as she tried to fit von Claus's kidnapping into a plausible version of the theory that Gambit had put forward.

73

But there was no way in which the presence of the Doctor would fit. The only connection was the fact that he was a German—but his record was impeccable. He had been a young man during the war and he had been imprisoned in a work camp rather than don the Nazi uniform. Though he had been qualified as a doctor and a biologist, he had refused even to do experiments on the inmates of the camp he was in. There seemed to be no connection at all between the flight of ADLER K7 and this Doctor von Claus.

While these thoughts were running through her head, Main followed her closely through the darkness.

The object of Steed and Purdey's search was trying to sleep in the cell that he had been given at the monastery. He was less unhappy than he had been earlier in the day—the fact of his kidnapping being alleviated by the success of the operation he had been asked to perform. He had long wanted to try the experiment on a human being, but had never dared risk such a move. The laws of scientific research and the disciplines involved were too strict for that.

He had eaten a light but satisfying supper with Father Trasker in the latter's private quarters and had allowed himself to be persuaded to take his boat back to the mainland in the morning rather than that night. Now, after some initial insomnia, he had at last slipped away into peaceful rest.

Karl came hurrying down the corridor to the Doctor's cell. He flung open the door and urgently shook the shoulder of the man in the bed. 'Doctor von Claus... Doctor von Claus...'

Von Claus was jerked into an unprepared wakefulness. He looked around him and gasped, unsure for the moment of where he was. It seemed as if he were in prison, but the man who was urgently shaking him awake wore the habit of a monk. A moment more and memory flooded back. He asked thickly, 'What is the matter?'

Karl's voice sounded close to tears in his panic and anxiety. 'He's not responding, Doctor. He has suffered a relapse.'

Von Claus leaped out of bed at once and began to dress feverishly, donning trousers, shirt and shoes—all he would need besides the surgically sterile equipment he would wear, and, at the same time divesting himself of the strange, old-fashioned nightshirt that Father Trasker had given him from his own wardrobe.

Karl was impatient and, as soon as the Doctor was dressed enough, he almost pushed him through the door, out into the corridor. They moved along as the Doctor buttoned his trousers, down the corridor, into the Great Hall and through the double doors to the corridor that housed the cell where McKay was lying.

Karl opened the door and went in ahead of Doctor von Claus. On the heart machine the Doctor noticed that the trace and beat were faint and spasmodic. He glanced at the body. It was lying as it had been left, in its packing of now half-melted ice. The only difference was that it was swathed so that most of the face and body was no longer visible.

Von Claus glanced at the body, his face reflecting his disbelief at the sudden deterioration of the man's life signs. He moved around the room making a quick check of the equipment, paying special attention to the pacemaker. At last, he muttered, 'The pacemaker is working perfectly—then why?'

He returned to the body in the coffin and looked down at the swathed figure. Then he leaned forward, undid the thermal clothing and placed one hand inside, on to the man's chest.'

Karl was quickly at his side. 'He's lapsed back into coma?'
'I'm afraid so.'

The Doctor withdrew his hand and Karl took it, begging as he spoke.

'But surely, we can go through the whole process again, can't we? He's still alive.'

The Doctor frowned. Something was troubling him, but Karl went on, 'Doctor, I am ready to go through the whole technique again—I am ready at any time.'

Von Claus remained silently thoughtful. He withdrew his hand from the other man's grip and turned back to the swaddled man. This time he lifted an arm slightly in order to check the man's wrist pulse. At the same moment he noticed that the hand was different—there was a ring on the man's little finger—a ring that had on it the seal of the head of an eagle, the sign of the Nazi elite.

That sight caused him to stare at the hand, and he saw that it was different, older and more gnarled. He swung round on Karl. 'This is not the same man.'

Karl tried the line of conciliation and argument. Insinuating himself between the Doctor and the patient, he said, 'Doctor von Claus—how could that possibly be?'

The Doctor shook his head, adamant. 'I said that this is not the same man.'

Karl was still whiningly obsequious. 'You are exhausted after your experiences and the operation, Doctor—perhaps if you were to rest for a little longer—I can maintain watch here an . . .'

'Show me the man's face,' thundered von Claus.

'Doctor.'

'I said show me his face.'

He saw that Karl was not going to step aside. He came forward and pushed the other man out of the way. He reached down and grabbed at the swaddling cloth, pulling it aside. For a moment he looked down, then froze in shock and horror at what he saw. He was so profoundly shocked, that he staggered away, only stopping when his back reached the wall of the cell. At the same moment Father Trasker came in. Doctor von Claus glanced up at him and managed to mutter, 'Oh, my God.'

But it was a very different Father Trasker to whom he spoke. No longer the gentle looking Abbot, Father Trasker stood tall, his eyes burning, a murderous Luger pistol in his hand. 'No, Doctor von Claus—*my* God.'

He came forward and struck the Doctor hard across the side of the face with his pistol so that the man fell with a moan to the cold stone floor, and lay, rocking to and fro, as much from the shock of what he had seen as from the pain of the blow.

Purdey came through the bushes to the outer wall of the monastery. She moved slowly away from the front of the building, until she came to the archway that led into the stable yard. She crept inside it and round the inner wall, trying each door cautiously as she went. At last she came round to one that was open, and slipped inside. She found herself in a dimly lit corridor. There was nothing ahead of her. She went forward and came to a bend, where she rested and waited. In the distance, she could hear the sound of a voice raised in anger, then louder as a door was opened. There was a cry and somebody fell. Slowly she inched her way round the corner and towards the sound of the fight.

Karl came round the side of the sick man's coffin bed and grabbed Trasker's arm as he prepared to hit Doctor von Claus again. 'Trasker, stop it.'

The other man tried to shake him off, shouting "This is foolishness—we need him unharmed. He has got to perform the operation for us.'

Trasker stepped back, under control, but not calm. Von Claus tried to rise and slumped back. He shrank away as Karl leaned forward to help him to his feet. Karl stood back and Trasker snapped, 'It is just as well that the Doctor knows just how determined we are. You will do as we say, Doctor, whatever your misguided feeling in the matter of the patient.'

Von Claus groaned and shook his head. 'It is hideous— obscene.'

'It is the future.'

Von Claus shouted, 'It is the past. A past to let die. I will not help you.' .

Trasker was once more above him. 'To let die? You blaspheme.'

Karl once more intervened to drag the older man away, but Trasker shook off his arm. His eyes were blazing with fanaticism. 'It is a pity, Doctor, that you saw through our little deception—had it worked, you might now have been on your way home and none the wiser. But now you must stay, and work to our orders.'

Von Claus managed to struggle to his feet. He was still dazed and he swayed on his feet before clutching the wall to hold himself up with one hand, while the other went to his bruised face. 'You will have to kill me first. I will never do this thing for you.'

Trasker suddenly smiled. 'Kill you? You are utterly indispensable, Doctor. We cannot kill you.'

He put such emphasis on the final word that the Doctor looked at him sharply and saw in his eyes that he was the mouse and that the other man was like a huge cat, playing with him.

'What do you mean?'

Trasker's voice was very low and filled with menace. 'As I said, Doctor, we cannot kill you. It is only you who can perform the operation we need. But you do have a wife—and three very lovely young daughters...'

'But they are...' The Doctor allowed his voice to trail away.

Trasker smiled grimly. 'Yes, you were going to say that they are in Germany. But we still have a few friends left in Germany when we need them. You understand?'

Von Claus tried to meet the other man's blazing eyes, but could not. His head hung down and Trasker went on smoothly, 'You see then—the matter is concluded. You have absolutely no other choice but to accede to our wishes.'

He turned towards the door, gesturing Karl to help the Doctor after them. Outside the door, Purdey, who had been a witness to the last part of the conversation, backed down the corridor to the bend, unaware of any danger from behind her. She watched as first Trasker, then Doctor von Claus, then the man supporting him left the cell and started down the corridor in the opposite direction. As the three men reached the studded door that led to the Great Hall, Trasker turned on his prisoner.

'We will move the patient back to his own special quarters—quarters more fitting to a person of such rank and intellect. In a little while you will conduct your first examination there.'

The men moved on out of sight and Purdey once more started forward after them, her ballet shoes making no noise on the stone floor. She edged very slowly along the corridor as she had before and, after a few infinitely long minutes she reached the doors themselves.

It was at that moment that Main, behind her, made his move and she realised why the island guards all carried fishing rods. She heard a whistling sound behind her and then the release of pressure as part of her suit was torn by her right shoulder.

She turned to face her attacker and saw that Main was at the far end of the corridor through which she had come, reeling in his line, the unbarbed hook on the end, and preparing for another cast. For a moment she was nonplussed as to how to deal with this form of attack and stood still long enough for him to make another cast.

Once again, there came the whistling noise as the line curled through the air and, this time, Purdey looked down in surprise as the rip in her shoulder was enlarged and the sleeve of her wet suit was split open down to the cuff.

Main smiled at her as she stood still, unable to make any defensive movement, and reeled in for yet another cast. This time, the hook whistled down and the front of her suit split open almost to the belted waist. Automatically, she clutched at the material to hold it together. She was angry as well as frightened—remembering how Stannard had died, from a small nick in his cheek that might have been caused by the unbarbed hook such as Main was using while he tormented her.

He reeled in again and this time, she was galvanised into action. He was preparing for yet another cast and she started to run for him down the corridor, hoping to get close enough for the rod and line to become too unwieldy to use at close quarters.

She was half way down the corridor when he made the new cast. The hook just grazed the back of the hand that was holding the wet suit together. She glanced down without faltering and saw the tiny speck of blood on her hand. Then she felt herself go dizzy.

As Main watched her, the smile still set on his face, the pleasure at her fear and discomfiture shining from his eyes, she faltered—stumbled, tried to right herself. Then her eyes glazed over and she fell unconscious to the floor.

Her tormentor moved forward until he was standing over her. He was wearing jackboots and, now that there was no need for caution, these rang out with each pace on the stones of the corridor.

Steed sat in the darkness on the edge of his bed. He was fully dressed but for his jacket and bowler hat, which lay on the bed beside him. Instinct had told him that something would happen that night and, at the sound of feet in the darkened village street, he was pleased to hear that his instinct was about to be rewarded.

To the first, single lone walker, he had paid no heed. But then these footsteps were joined by a second and then by a third and then more, as if a growing crowd were going from house to house, collecting more of their number as they went.

As the footsteps came nearer to the side of the inn, as if making for the narrow road that led up to the monastery, Steed moved cautiously forward and opened the curtains the tiniest crack to look down.

He gasped involuntarily at the sight that met his eyes. It looked as if a great line of monks, all with their cowls up, was moving forward up the road, their way lit only by the flaming brand that the lead monk carried in his hand. They marched in a perfect line—like a well-trained army of worker ants, all intent upon the threat ahead of them.

Steed let out a low whistle. 'That's my clue to the monkey business.'

He turned away from the window and silently slipped on his jacket, before putting his bowler hat on at a jaunty angle. Then he went quietly to the door and out into the hall closing it equally softly behind him. He waited a moment, but could hear nothing. As far as he could ascertain, he was not being watched.

He crept slowly down the corridor to the stairs. Once again, at the head of them, he blended back into the shadows and waited for almost a full minute to make sure that his was the only presence at the top of the stairs.

Satisfied, he started slowly down. There were the inevitable creaks in the stairs, but he felt they were unobtrusive enough not to warn anyone who might be lying in wait for him at the bottom—provided they did not live on a diet consisting almost entirely of carrots. He couldn't see a thing, but to someone like that, his presence could be as plain as day.

He was still in the midst of this irrelevant thought when he reached the bend in the stairs and froze again. Somewhere below him a door opened and closed, then the lights in the bar were switched on. The landlord, Jud, appeared in his line of vision, making for the bar. He might be there for hours. There was no way to get past him. Steed felt he must take a chance and bluff it out.

The landlord bent down and came up again clutching a brown robe—a monk's habit. Steed felt that the moment was right, so he straightened up, began to hum loudly and advanced down the stairs making the normal amount of clatter that an innocent man makes when going out at two in the morning for a constitutional.

The landlord glanced up and reacted by dropping the brown robe behind the bar. 'Mr Steed!'

Steed strode casually up to the bar as if he didn't have a care or suspicion in the world. As he leaned across it with an avuncular smile, the flustered landlord went on, 'I'd've thought you'd have been asleep by now, sir.'

Steed gave his bravest smile, knowing how much it would irritate the impatient man in front of him. 'Couldn't sleep—too much noise outside. I must say this village is a busy place at night. A stroll outside might help, I think.'

The man looked alarmed. It might have been Steed's imagination, but he seemed to pale slightly in the artificial light of the bar.

'Oh, I wouldn't do that, sir.'

Steed beamed. 'Very thoughtful of you, landlord. I mean, worrying after your guests' health and all that. Not to worry though. Mummy's let me go out at night for years. I can always wrap up well.'

As he spoke, Steed could see that the man was reaching under the bar for something. He prayed inwardly that it was some sort of cosh—if the man had a gun there he might just have the advantage. He added, 'What was all the noise about, by the way?'

The landlord looked flustered. 'Ummm—it was the fishing boats coming in. Always do at this time of night.'

Steed frowned. 'Funny. The harbour must be bigger than I thought. It was jam-packed with boats when I went for a stroll before dark. They must be queueing up for moorings now, don't you think?'

The landlord muttered, 'It is a chill night, sir.'

Steed took his elbows off the bar and half turned towards the door. Inwardly he was as tense as a coiled spring—outwardly he seemed perfectly relaxed. As he took his first pace away, he said, 'Don't worry—I have a very warm nature.'

He took another pace, then heard the sound as the man withdrew a baulk of wood to use as a cosh from under the bar. The landlord was fast with it, but John Steed was faster. He swept his bowler hat off his head and slammed the landlord across the forehead with the brim. There was a metallic clang as the bowler hit its target, the landlord's eyes rolled up in his head and the cosh dropped with a satisfyingly painful noise on his foot as he fell.

Steed placed the life-saving and versatile bowler hat on the bar, then walked round it to pick up the monk's robe. As he did so, he murmured with a smile, 'My mother always said I would fall into bad habits.'

He put it on over his suit, then added the bowler before putting the cowl up. The general effect was most unsatisfactory, so, reluctantly he replaced the bowler back in its place on the bar, and pulled the cowl up to cover his face.

The village outside was now quiet and deserted. He swore at the indulgence he had allowed himself in wasting so much time on the landlord and stumbled in the dark up the road towards the monastery. He could only hope that he would not be too late to join the other 'monks' at whatever peculiar devotions they were attending.

He was in luck. The line of monks was still moving up the last few hundred yards of road to the monastery. He hurried silently up in the shadows at the side of the path, then joined on to the end of the line. It took him a moment or two to get the hang of the pace, but eventually he was in step, without the man in front of him being disturbed by the sudden appearance of a new end to the line. Presumably they thought it was their esteemed landlord joining them after locking up.

The doors of the monastery were open and the monks poured in, still keeping to their disciplined file. They went in at one end of the building and down the corridor to the Main Hall. Steed noticed as he went along the corridor, the cell doors, some of them with the bolts drawn back, some of them bolted up.

Going down the corridor, he passed closer to Purdey than he might have guessed. She had been taken from the stone corridor, along, through the Main Hall and into this other corridor where she had been flung down on a pallet bed in one of the cells. She had been left there for a while, then Main had gone back. He had sat on a chair by her bed and had dangled the rod in front of her, the unbarbed fish-hook inches from her face. He smiled down, knowing it was only a matter of moments before she would awaken from the drug with which he had baited his hook.

He had timed the awakening almost to the exact moment. He watched as she opened first one eye, then the other, then, blinking rapidly to overcome the dizziness, both eyes. Only then, as she focused on the hook dangling in front of her face did he speak. 'You're lucky.'

With some difficulty, Purdey transferred her gaze from focusing on the hook to trying to make out the speaker. At first he was a blur, then came slowly into focus as her senses returned. She absorbed his remark and glanced round the bare, white-walled cell. 'I am?'

Main nodded. 'We bait our hooks either to kill or to stun. Luckily for you I fancied using the latter tonight.'

'Why tonight?' She knew the answer from the look on his face before the question was out of her mouth.

He smiled.

'Because I fancied . . . other things . . .'

She tried to make light of his remark, while conscious that the ripped wet suit was more of a provocation than a protection in its present state.

'Naughty—but I know the feeling.'

His smile intensified into something less healthy. 'You do?'

'Well, fancying things—I mean, right at this moment, I fancy a steak au poivre—preferably at the George Cinq in Paris—do you think you could possibly make the arrangements?'

As she spoke, she looked up at him coquettishly and the smile vanished from his face as he realised that she was defying him and sneering at him. He stepped forward and pressed the end of the fishing rod at the side of her face.

'Quiet. I have some questions.'

'Fire ahead. But I'm not very hot on general knowledge.'

The rod was pressed a little more but she ignored the pain.

'When did you come ashore?' he snapped.

'Come ashore? But I came over just like anyone else on the ferry. You must have seen me land?'

He shook his head. 'Try again. I want answers.'

She was silent and he removed the rod. For a moment she thought she would have a respite but he merely wanted to crouch down by the bed—to pick up the flippers she had so carefully concealed in the bushes near O'Hara's cottage. The rod was replaced and he once more leered down at her, holding up the offending objects.

'We found these—now when and why?'

'Ah, yes—those. Well, you may find this a bit difficult to believe—but I can't remember.'

Once more the rod was pressed into the side of her face. Purdey began to think that if she didn't do something about his obnoxious behaviour, she was going to collect a really nasty bruise mark that would keep her out of the social whirl for days.

Main said, 'I asked you when and why?'

Purdey let her eyes glaze and roll up in her head for a moment as if she were fainting. At once the pressure of the rod was removed. Her tormentor wasn't so clever and sure of himself after all. She allowed herself to move slightly so that the rent in the front of her suit was just that much more revealing. He was easily distracted.

'I can't . . . can't remember a thing.'

'What do you mean?'

She looked up at him again, coy appeal on her face. 'I must have bumped my head or something.'

He was leering down at her, torn between admiration for the lines of her body and anger at the fact that she was making a fool out of him and he knew it.

Purdey prattled on. 'But thanks so much for looking after me—putting me up and all that, i'm so grateful.'

He was silent as he observed her and she slowly rose from the bed. The torn suit was a very useful distraction.

'Now I really must be going.'

Inwardly, she sighed. The suit was not as big a distraction as she had calculated. He quickly barred her way to the door, his face suffused once more with anger.

'Sit down.'

She backed away and sat on the edge of the bed, trying at the same time to look her most appealing.

'I knew you wouldn't believe me. All you men are the same.'

For an answer, he glanced at his watch. 'I have to go now. There are things to be done. I will be back later—and then we will see just how co-operative you are.'

The door closed on him and she heard the bolts being shot home. She glanced round and saw that there was really no adequate hope of escape from the cell, so she lay down on the bed. If there was no reason to expend energy on futile attempts to deal with the door, then now was the time to rest and ready herself for the moment an opportunity presented itself.

The monks had now all reached the Main Hall. On one end a dais had been placed and on the dais stood Father Trasker, watching the monks as they shuffled in and took up their position in straight ranks in front of him, their cowls still covering their heads.

Behind the dais was a huge version of the Nazi eagle motif and the Father presented an incongruous figure in front of it, or so Steed thought as he came into line in the back row, and space was made for him by the other monks in the row.

With these final movements a great silence fell on the room, a silence that brooded and hung over the assembled company. It was broken as Main joined the others and closed the great doors at the end of the hall, so that the room was closed. Steed kept as calm as he could. Whatever transpired in this room, he was trapped.

Father Trasker stepped forward to the edge of the dais and pushed back his cowl, baring the great mane of white hair. His face was grim, his eyes a flashing blue as he stared down at them. When he spoke his voice was as hard as his exterior. 'Brothers. Brothers of St Dorca, welcome.'

The monks bowed to this greeting and Steed followed suit. He had a moment of doubt—perhaps he had just butted in on the rituals of a fanatical island-wide religious sect—or even a bingo coven—but the man's next words told him that he had been right to be suspicious.

'Tomorrow, as you well know, is the twentieth of April—a day of birth and rebirth.'

There was a murmur among the monks and Trasker silenced it with a basilisk stare. 'Brothers. Please. On April 20th 1889, there came among us a man who was to change the face of the world—he is still with us.'

Father Trasker paused to let the import of his words sink in. Under his cowl, Steed frowned, then almost gasped out loud at the significance of what he was hearing.

The man on the dais went on, 'Tomorrow—on the very day of his birth—he will be restored to us. I ask you all now to

85

honour him. I ask you to cast aside the trappings we have presented as a face to the outside world for so long—cast them aside and stand proudly as we most truly are.'

As he spoke, he undid the front of his habit and let it fall from his shoulders to the ground. Steed's mouth fell open as he saw something similar to what he might have expected—Trasker was dressed in the full dress uniform of a senior SS Officer.

There was a silence and stillness in the hall, then, one by one, the monks began to shed their own habits to reveal that they too were dressed—to a man and woman—in Nazi uniforms, complete with all the regalia that went with them. Steed noticed that all the men and women he had seen in the village were there—the whole island.

Trasker raised his hand in the Nazi salute. 'Heil!'

'Heil . . . Heil . . . Heil . . .'

The cry was taken up until it filled the whole room. Steed stood at the back. No one had yet noticed that he was still wearing his monk's habit, the cowl still covering his head and face.

On the dais, Trasker began to sing the first words of the Horst Wessel song—stamping his jackbooted foot to indicate the timing. The song was taken up all round the room and was in full swing when, quite suddenly, Trasker stopped and came to attention, staring down the length of the Great Hall. The sounds of singing died away until the room was silent again and one by one the other occupants of the room turned in the direction in which he was staring.

They were all looking at Steed, standing in their midst, still in the habit of a monk of St Dorca, his cowl up. He shrugged and removed the cowl. Then he held up one hand in a limp and apologetic gesture.

'Rule Britannia?'

Chapter Six

Considering the odds against him and the circumstances of his discovery in their midst, Steed felt that the enemies among whom he had been uncovered had given him a pretty gentle time as they took him into custody.

He was lifted off his feet and rushed from the Main Hall, down the corridor, and was then steered into a cell where he was dumped unceremoniously on the bed. His captors then retreated, slammed the cell door and he heard the bolts go home. It took him a few moments to relieve himself of the monk's habit, before he was able to sit on the edge of the bed, get his bearing and take in his surroundings in order to plan how he would go out among his enemies again.

It was a moment before he realised that the faint tapping he could hear was not inside his head, but was coming from the wall by the bed—and thus presumably from the cell next to his—or some space between the two cells.

He put his ear to the wall and heard someone faintly calling his name.

'Steed . . . Steed . . .'

It was Purdey's voice and he shouted back, 'Purdey. Thank goodness you're around. Now stir your stumps and get me out of here. I don't think they like me very much.'

There was an explosion of muffled sound from the wall, in the midst of which Steed could have sworn he heard what he might have described as a muffled oath, then the voice came clear again.

'Get you out—I'm in the cell next door.'

He thought about this for a moment. 'Oh, dear. It seems I'm going to have to rethink our whole strategy. We seem to have made fools of ourselves.'

This last remark was greeted both by the wall and by his confrere behind it in stony silence. Just as he was beginning to think that Purdey had lost interest in his predicament altogether and had wandered away, he heard her voice once more. 'What's going on, Steed?'

He laughed. 'Well, you may not believe this—but I think we are the prisoners of the SS.'

'The SS?'

'I wish I knew what was going on Purdey. April 1889—von Claus kidnapped. I'm not sure how it all links up.'

He heard her laugh.

'Well, when you get a line on it—could you please let me know?'

After this exchange, there didn't seem to be anything more to say, so Steed settled down to working out how he was going to escape—or if he was.

In a chamber in the inner part of the monastery, Doctor von Claus was getting a run down on just the mysteries that Steed and Purdey wanted to discover. With the greatest reluctance, but fearing for the safety of his wife and children, von Claus was going along with his captors, but as slowly and unwillingly as possible.

As he worked, checking over the equipment for the operation he was being forced to perform, Trasker told him about the flight of DER ADLER K7 and its strange destination. He asked, 'You were one of the original group who came here?'

Trasker nodded. 'There were forty-two of us aboard the aircraft when it crash-landed here—men and women—all of us dedicated Nazis—all of us dedicated to the service of the Führer.'

'But a whole island—how did you manage to take over a whole island?'

'It was not so difficult. We almost outnumbered the local population. All the young men of the island were away—either fighting in the war or on essential war work on the mainland. We had just the women and children and a few old men to overcome.'

'And how did you "overcome" them?'

'Those who submitted to our will were permitted to survive, they are, after all, good Aryan stock.'

Von Claus sneered. 'And the rest, I suppose, were slaughtered?'

Trasker nodded. 'Or they were used for certain experiments we had to make—the end justifies the means.'

Doctor von Claus shook his head sadly and said in a voice that was heavy with bitterness, 'Yes. I understand. That battle cry has been responsible for much of the slaughter and bloodshed that has taken place in the world one way or another through the centuries.'

Trasker seemed to ignore the reproof. 'This island is ours now, Doctor. Over the years we have populated and controlled it—it is ours now.'

'The last bastion of Nazi Germany.'

To his surprise, Trasker smiled as he shook his head. 'No, Doctor, not the last bastion—the first. From here, we will spread and grow and conquer again.' His hand went to the Doctor's shoulder and he added more confidentially, 'With your professional assistance, of course, Doctor.'

Their eyes met. Von Claus went on testing the hypodermic he had picked up and Trasker grabbed him by the wrist, hurting him so that he winced and nearly dropped it.

'Don't even think it, Doctor. Karl will be here watching your every move. You make the wrong one—you even hesitate for an instant—then I must remind you to think of your wife and three pretty daughters.'

Gambit came out of the water in his wet suit at the deserted village. He came up on to the quay and looked around. Everything seemed too silent for comfort. He took off his flippers and replaced them with soft shoes from inside the wet suit, then padded over to the inn where he knew that Steed was staying. He tried the handle to the bar door and was surprised and suspicious when it just swung open. That was not a natural phenomenon in a Scottish pub at two o'clock in the morning.

As the door swung completely open, he rolled in and came up to the crouch in the darkness, his automatic in his hand. The precautions were greeted with almost complete silence. Somewhere in the room with him, someone was breathing stertorously, as if they were asleep.

He moved slowly and carefully until he came to the side of the room, felt along the wall and found the light switch. He snapped it on and found himself staring straight down at the landlord, now sleeping peacefully after his brush with Steed. The reason for his deep sleep was evident on the bar—Steed's specially reinforced bowler hat. Gambit grinned, walked over and picked it up. He had a chance to do something he had always wanted to do. He flung the bowler across the room like a frisbee. It hit the far wall with a metallic clang and fell to the floor. After a moment there came a series of static noises, then the hat started to play pleasant light music to the occupants of the bar.

Steed himself had not been long in thought for a solution to his problem when the tapping came once more on the wall. Purdey called, 'Steed?'

'Yes.'

'They'll probably kill us, won't they?'

Steed sighed but kept his voice cheerful. 'I do fear that they have something rather permanent in mind—yes.'

There was a long silence, then Purdey said shakily, 'Steed?'

'Yes?'

'I . . . I want to confess . . .'

Steed was alarmed. 'Steady on, dear. The habit was just a disguise to get me in here, you know.'

She went on as if she hadn't heard him. 'I don't really think that you're like St Paul's Cathedral at all.'

'What?'

She rushed on breathless with embarrassment. 'Gambit used to think that you were old-fashioned—But I used to say, well, suppose you are—so is St Paul's. And you've both survived a long time.'

Steed didn't quite know how to take this last remark. Was it a compliment or an insult? He was just thinking out a suitable answer that would not make him sound either stupid or condescending when he froze at the sound of his door being unbolted.

He turned as a man in monk's robes, his cowl pulled up over his head, entered the room and snapped, 'Stand up. You are to be executed immediately.'

Steed stood up very slowly, mustering all his dignity, looking as if the news meant no more to him than a message that his suit was back from the dry cleaners. He even managed a smile as he turned. 'Well, thank goodness you broke it to me gently. I think we should always be straightforward about such things.'

The man was surprised by this reaction and Steed gave him no time of reflection. He brought his heels together with a sudden click and raised his arm. 'Heil.'

Like one of Pavlov's dogs, the man reacted with a similar gesture—raising his right hand, in which he was also carrying a gun. 'Heil.'

Steed moved his left hand faster than the man could see. The gun hit the floor and his jaw snapped at the same time. Then he went down like a sack of coals. Steed picked him up by the shoulders and dragged him to the bed. He made a half-hearted attempt to lift him up on it, decided that he was too heavy for such an unnecessary effort and instead rolled him under the bed. He scooped up the gun and sauntered out into the corridor, ready to shoot first and ask questions afterwards.

Purdey heard the bolts being drawn back on the door to her cell and assumed gloomily that she was about to endure another pointless session of question and answer with Main. She could not believe her eyes when her visitor proved to be Steed— suddenly no longer captive—and miraculously carrying a gun.

'How?'

Steed shrugged airily. 'Just one of those old-fashioned tricks. Time and experience, that's what does it.'

She laughed and rose to join him, holding her suit together as decently as she could. He raised an eyebrow.

'Well, if you think you're dressed for it, I think it's about time we found out a bit more about what's going on in these hallowed walls.'

They went back into the corridor, then crept along, apparently undetected, into the Main Hall. They moved quickly across it to the great studded doors at the far end. Steed hit the door with the flat of his hand.

'Whatever is going on—is going on in there.'

He gripped the gun firmly, then his free hand went cautiously for the door handle. If there were an armed guard on the far side of the door who had been wily enough not to come out at his knock, then his position would be a dangerous one.

He was about to turn the handle when he received a nudge in the ribs from Purdey. He turned and immediately moved away from the door, gun in hand. Main, Gunner and two other men had entered the Great Hall and were slowly advancing on the fugitives. There was a smile of confidence on Main's face and he and Gunner both held fishing rods on which were the unbarbed hooks.

Steed snapped, 'I'd advise you to stay where you are. I abhor violence and gunshots make me blink.'

Still they came on.

'Sorry about this.'

He squeezed the trigger as the men came closer. There was a dull click and nothing else. Steed and Purdey exchanged glances of mutual apology. As they did so there came the familiar whistling sound and the gun was jerked out of Steed's hand by Main's fishing line.

Steed stared at his hand with exaggerated astonishment. Main and Gunner both laughed, stood their ground and prepared to cast in unison. Steed kept his head slightly lowered as if he could still not believe that the gun was no longer in his hand. As for Purdey she made no movement but to rise up on point in her ballet shoes.

Main picked her for his target. As he made his cast and the line whistled forward, Purdey moved towards him, took the impact of the line on her side, then went in to a pirouetting spin like a ballerina, with the line wrapping round her until she was up with and facing Main. As she reached that optimum position, one graceful leg flashed out and took him under the chin, knocking him backwards down the room.

At the same time, Gunner made his cast. Steed stepped gracefully to one side, grabbed the line and jerked it out of the other man's hands. Gunner did not let go quite soon enough and the impetus that Steed's jerk gave him brought him up the room to collide with him. Gunner fell away, leaving Steed holding the line and the rod. As he started to reel in, he watched with amazement as Purdey continued to deal with Main.

He was beginning to get back to his feet and she made another balletic spin towards him. He was half way up when the elegant foot was there again, perfectly placed to clobber him on the jaw with the first spin, then full in the face as she came round again.

He was staggering purposelessly now and she abruptly stopped the spin, facing him. The leg came up and took him under the chin with such force that, not only did Steed hear his jaw click as it broke, but he was lifted off his feet and sent crashing and sliding against the far wall where, with great presence of mind and self-preservation, he fell unconscious and lay still.

Steed was still staring at the result of Purdey's prowess when Gunner came back into the fray. He rushed at the unprepared man, but Purdey was more than ready for him. She leapt from her toes position, landing lightly by the attacking man, did a fast back kick that sent him spinning, then crossed his eyes with a neat right hand as she spun round. He folded up like an old rug and hit the floor. Purdey turned towards Steed and ended her dance of mayhem with a low curtsy, arms outstretched for applause.

Steed could only stare before asking, 'Where the hell did you learn all that—the Marine Commandos?'

She stood, remembered her torn suit and covered herself demurely, before shaking her head. 'Royal Ballet. They threw me out.'

Steed shouted, 'They threw you out? What did you do—maim the male lead during his pas de deux?'

Purdey glared him down. 'Too tall.'

She walked back across the room to pick up the fallen gun.

As she bent for it, there came the familiar whistling sound and the gun was pulled out from under her hand. She turned quickly to see Steed grasping the butt, a satisfied smile on his face. It was her turn to look at him with admiration.

'Wow.'

Steed shrugged modestly and Purdey asked, 'Where did you learn that—the Slade School?'

Steed looked at his fingernails. 'The result of a misspent youth. Poached salmon was always my favourite dish, next to tickled trout.'

The two of them took a moment or two to recover, then Steed once more made for the studded door at the end of the hall, opened it and slipped through into the corridor beyond, Purdey silently on his heels.

Beyond this door was a short corridor. Another door was open at the far end and they could hear the murmur of voices from it as soon as they were in the corridor. They moved cautiously towards it, then entered with a quick, abrupt movement, stopping dead the moment they did so at the sight that met their eyes.

The room was like a vast shrine to Nazi regalia—all of it centering on the incongruous operating table in the centre. Von Claus and Karl were bent over the strange coffin-like container, working on the patient. Trasker stood near by watching them, his back to the door.

At the moment of their entry, von Claus had a needle lifted high.

'The direct injection into the heart.'

'We are just seconds away,' said Karl, his voice filled with excitement.

As he spoke, he glanced round at the waiting Trasker, then froze as he became aware of the two newcomers in the doorway. The other two men turned towards the door and also saw Steed and Purdey. Steed lifted the gun. Empty or not, he would have to bluff it out.

'Please, gentlemen.'

Trasker and Karl both froze. Von Claus still stood at the site of his operation, the hypodermic in his hand.

Steed went on, 'Doctor von Claus. I do not know why you are here—but I suspect it is under duress? Would you kindly step to one side? You might get in the line of fire if there is any trouble.'

Von Claus started to back away from the strange operating table, but Karl intervened, turning and glaring at him. 'No.'

There was real fear in von Claus's face as he froze beneath the other man's stare.

'Please?'

Karl snarled at him, 'But he will die.' He turned to Steed. 'If you stop this operation now, a man will die.'

Steed was a bit thrown by this announcement. He turned his attention to von Claus. 'Is that true, Doctor?'

Reluctantly the kidnapped biologist nodded. 'There is a man in a coma here, yes.'

Steed snapped, 'How did it happen—and when?'

'He has been in a coma since April 1945—injuries received as the result of an air crash.'

Steed raised his eyebrows. 'That's a dreadful time to be in a coma. Please continue.'

This time it was von Claus who did not move. There was a mixture of fear and pleading in his eyes as he looked at the man with a gun. 'You have not yet seen who the man is.'

'Is that important? It is a life.'

Von Claus beckoned them forward. 'You must see for yourselves.'

Steed glanced at Purdey, then moved forward, the girl following a careful distance behind him, never for a moment taking her eyes off Trasker and Karl, who returned her glances with stares of baleful and impotent hatred. As Steed walked past Trasker he saw the Luger in the other man's hand and reacted to the sight of it.

Steed and Purdey reached the side of the ice-container. They gazed in at a man dressed completely in a thermal suit, the chest open, the head hidden by the swaddling surrounding it— comatose—unmoving.

Purdey gasped, 'He is dead.'

Von Claus shook his head sadly. 'Regrettably, no. Comatose. In a state of suspended animation. Every organ in his body preserved—kept artificially alive.'

Steed shuddered fastidiously. 'Every organ. What a way not to go.'

Von Claus leaned forward and pulled back the swaddling that covered the face causing Purdey and Steed to gasp with shock as the man's identity was revealed to them. He looked just as he had in his photographs, the cowlick of hair on the forehead, the little toothbrush moustache. Steed gasped.

'Germany's greatest treasure.'

Von Claus nodded gravely. 'Nazi Germany. You see now why I am so grateful for your intrusion.'

From behind them, Trasker's voice rasped, 'You will continue, Herr Doctor.'

Steed and Purdey both whirled round as von Claus looked up at the man who had spoken. He was now holding in his hand a long-nosed Mauser pistol. Steed raised his own gun as a reminder. Though it was empty, he could still hope to bluff out the other man. It was a hope that Trasker quickly dashed.

'The gun you hold is a Luger—it was taken, I believe, from one of my more careless men. Ammunition has been a precious commodity here for many years.'

Steed did not let the flicker of an eyelid betray him, but kept holding the Luger up firmly as a counter from the Mauser the other man held—a gun, which, by implication, was a sight more lethal than his own.

Trasker went on with calm confidence, 'We have had time to devise other ways of killing—and the gun remains as merely a method of intimidation. They are rarely loaded, but this one is. One must take certain precautions. There is always the unthinkable to consider in any situation.'

With that, he ignored Steed and turned his attention to von Claus.

'You will please continue, Herr Doctor. Restore our glorious leader to us—so that he may lead us again. This time it will surely be to victory. Continue, Herr Doctor. Complete your work.'

His shoulder hunched in despair, Doctor von Claus turned reluctantly back to his patient, while Steed and Purdey still held their ground, helpless but determined not to give in until they had to. All of them were frozen as a new voice said quietly from the doorway, 'This is a Smith and Wesson.'

Von Claus gasped as Karl and Trasker both whirled round to see the newcomer. There was no need for Steed and Purdey to look. Gambit's voice, at that moment, was the most welcome in the world. Even so, they could not resist turning slowly to acknowledge his presence.

He was crouched in the doorway, the gun held up, ready to fire. He said tightly, when he was sure that he had everyone's attention, 'It's a Magnum .38. I'll have no problems over ammunition. I loaded it myself this morning.'

Steed relaxed. There was no need for him to bluff any more. He cleared his throat. 'It seems we have a sort of stand-off, gentlemen. I would suggest that a parley is in order.'

Trasker's eyes blazed, but the gun in his hand did not waver for an instant from its new target—the crouching Gambit. 'Be quiet, Mr Steed.'

'Sorry, I'm sure.'

Trasker, after a moment's silence and still without taking his eyes from his armed opponent, snapped, 'Karl.'

'Yes.'

'I am holding a Mauser—a Mauser automatic.'

Gambit supplied the firearm details. 'Press the trigger and it fires the whole clip.'

Trasker smiled thinly. 'Precisely, sir. One bullet will surely find its mark—you must go on with the operation, Karl. It is important.'

Karl's voice was shaking, hardly above a whisper. 'Yes.'

'You promise me?'

'I promise.'

At Karl's words, something in Trasker relaxed, though the gun was still steady. He said softly, 'My life means nothing—but his is everything.'

With that, his finger squeezed on the trigger. Steed hurled the empty Luger at his hand. It hit the German and the latter's gun went off in what seemed to be the same moment. Steed's movement had been enough to deflect Trasker's aim by the necessary amount to make his shot pass Gambit and, a split second later, the Englishman fired, his bullet finding its target in the German's shoulder.

As he took the impact of the bullet, Trasker staggered backwards, half-falling, the arm holding the gun swinging wide, rattling off the whole clip of automatic shots.

Steed and Purdey hit the ground simultaneously. The bullets went over their heads and the trolley formed the main target. The glass and metal sides of the coffin in which Germany's Greatest Treasure reposed were shattered by the shots. Purdey swung round on the floor and sent the gun flying from Trasker's hand.

Karl was the first to move. He ran forward again to the trolley, pushing aside von Claus, who was crouched down beside it, frozen with fear. He stared down in horror at the patient, then screamed and sobbed.

Trasker, struggling against the effects of the wound he had suffered, the arm of his uniform sodden with blood, staggered back on to his feet and moved towards the trolley. He stared down into it at the comatose figure, his repose disturbed, then his distraught face turned to Karl and their eyes met.

Trasker saw the answer he sought in them and screamed, 'No...No...No.'

Then, strength ebbing out of him, he fell forward across the trolley of his leader and God, hiding the damage his bullets had done from the sight of the others.

Steed picked himself up and dusted himself down before helping Purdey to her feet. 'Are you all right?'

'Thank you, kind sir.'

They both turned to Gambit, who was coming slowly towards them, a grin of pleasure on his face. Steed gave him a mock glare.

'You were long enough in coming.'

Gambit nodded. 'Sorry about that. The man you left at the inn with the directions was a bit too preoccupied to tell me where you went.'

'All's well that ends well,' smiled Steed. 'I suppose you two had better see to the others.'

Purdey salaamed: 'Yes, O Master.'

While Purdey and Gambit searched the rest of the monastery for weapons and locked the other 'monks' into the cells that their enemies had so thoughtfully provided for such a purpose, Steed helped Doctor von Claus to patch up the wounded Trasker. Now that his master was dead, the former Abbot was just a shrivelled old man, almost as inert as his God had been for the past thirty years.

The next morning, shortly after dawn, Gambit, Steed and Purdey took the 'monks' from their cells and rounded them up into the Great Hall. With the weapons at their command and the demoralisation of their enemies, now that their cause was dead, they could see they would have no trouble with them.

'My colleagues will march you all down to the quay, from which you will take your boats and go to the mainland. There you will be dealt with by the local authorities,' Steed told them.

That was orders enough to deal with most of the 'monks'. It only left a small group consisting of Trasker, Karl and their closest henchmen to be escorted in a more personal fashion down to the village and thence to the mainland.

Von Claus went with Steed in the wake of this little party. As they walked down the road above the village, they could already see the boats containing the other islanders setting off for the mainland.

Von Claus said, 'I would never have forgiven myself if I had brought that demon back to life, Mr Steed.'

'It can never happen now, Doctor. By the way, do you want us to take you back to London?'

The Doctor shook his head. 'No. I must get back to Germany as soon as possible. My wife and daughters, they were under threat from those horrible men.'

Steed smiled. 'I think London would be better, Doctor. You've more chance of joining them there. I took the liberty of having Mr Gambit bring them back with him when he was in Germany yesterday—and I think you'll find them at their hotel waiting for you.'

Von Claus gasped. 'You mean, they have been under your protection—they were in no danger.'

Steed grinned and the Doctor grabbed his hand and shook it with such warmth that it was almost embarrassing to the

Englishman. They had reached the start of the village and Steed was able to break away and excuse himself by saying that he had to go to the inn to collect his luggage.

He had forgotten entirely about the landlord, and the condition he had left him in the night before. He pushed open the door to the bar and went inside. His bowler hat, he noted with some pain, was on the far side of the bar, the long-life transistor battery circuits that were part of its equipment still churning out pop music. He went over and picked it up, in order to change the frequency and transmit a message to the mainland about the sudden influx of prisoners that they could expect.

As he bent down to pick up the hat, he heard the slightest hint of noise behind him and, instead of straightening up fell flat to the floor. The baulk of wood with which the man had tried to attack him the night before, hit the wall above his head.

The pain to the man's wrists on bringing it into contact with something as hard as a stone wall, caused him to drop the baulk and scream out. Steed grabbed the bowler, swung round and threw it so that it hit the man full in the face. Once more, Steed took pleasure in seeing him unconscious before he hit the ground.

As for the bowler, it oscillated for a moment, then said, 'At the third stroke it will be 0 six fifty-six and thirty seconds . . . At the third stroke it will be . . .'

Steed picked up the offending example of technicalogical advance and switched it to transmitting frequencies, before relaying a message to the police on the mainland about the prisoners. He also had a message put through to Glasgow for relay to 'Mother' on the bodies and equipment that would have to be removed from the island. These jobs done, he put the bowler on his head at a rakish angle and made his way down to the quay. 'Mother's' people could take care of returning his luggage to London when they came.

Gambit was sitting on a bollard on the quay, his gun held carelessly in his hand as he watched the huddled group of cowed Germans on the boat in which he would be taking them into custody. Purdey was by his side and she smiled as Steed joined them.

'Are we ready to go?'

Gambit nodded, then laughed as Steed's bowler started making strange noises.

'Hadn't you better switch your hat off?'

Steed took off the bowler and pulled out the aerial. At once the voice of Morgan, one of the duty men in the radio room in London came through.

'Mr Steed?'

'Yes, Morgan, what is it?'

'Rostock's made contact, sir. Just his call sign and the code.'

'What does that mean?'

'It means he wants us to stand by—that he'll have an important message for us in the next twenty-four hours.'

Steed frowned. 'Thanks for letting us know. I'll be in London as soon as I can.'

He turned to the others. 'No peace for the wicked. We'd better get these people over and get back to London as fast as we can. If Rostock's in contact, it means something big is going on. I'll take the little motor-boat.'

Before Purdey or Gambit could protest, Steed had jumped into the motor-boat that had brought him to the island, had cast off and was drifting away from the quay as he started up. The engine took at once and he zoomed out of the harbour and made for the mainland.

As soon as he was out of sight of the island, he took the boat's speed down to a crawl, then once more fiddled with the transmission dials inside his hat. A voice said,

'AA radio telephone service.'

Steed asked for a number, waiting while he heard it ringing, then, when it was answered the other end, he said softly, 'Sara, my dear. I know you must think I'm talking through my hat after the last couple of weeks, but I'm coming back from Scotland tonight—why don't the two of us have a spot of dinner.'

He listened for a moment, then chuckled. 'That's wonderful. Then we can celebrate your birthday tonight. As a matter of fact I'm already celebrating someone else's—no, no one you know. He hasn't been too well of late, in fact he hasn't had a celebration for thirty years.'

He switched off his hat, put it back on his head and revved up the engine of the little boat again, to make for the mainland.

Chapter Seven

By evening, the file on what John Steed had chosen to call 'The Eagle's Nest' was closed, the report on its way to 'Mother' to go into the dead files. On their return to London, Steed had warned Purdey and Gambit that, while they could rest from their ordeal, they should remain within telephone distance. If Rostock came through that night as he had signalled, what he would have to say might be important enough to engage their attention.

As for himself, he spent the latter half of the afternoon submerged in the healing waters of a hot bath, before preparing himself for the assault of the evening—for dinner was only the first of the plans he had for Sara.

Across London, at the communications centre, Morgan had volunteered to do extra duty. He had monitored for Rostock for so long that he wanted to hear what the man had to say. At the point where Steed's plans were proceeding from oysters to roast beef in one of London's most fashionable restaurants, the frequency on which Morgan was listening sprang to life and began to bleep out its urgent message in morse code. There was no time for Morgan to do anything but a fast transcription—before the line and the frequency abruptly went dead, the message unfinished.

Morgan could only imagine what had happened. He had no way to see the tiny hut, the blizzard swirling round it in the Siberian wastes. Nor could he see Rostock's dead body or the men who stood over him, their machine-guns still at the ready. They were men who might easily pass for Russian border guards, but for the slanting of their eyes and the slightly Asiatic cast and colouring of their features.

Their leader glanced around the hut to make sure their work was done and, as an afterthought, put a burst of machine-gun fire through the transmitter, smashing it beyond repair. He and his fellows backed out of the hut into the blizzard, leaving the door open. Soon the snow would have covered everything, the hut would be frozen in, the evidence of their acts hidden perhaps for ever.

Steed still had no indication that Rostock had tried to make contact as he rose from the table and suggested to the beautiful woman facing him that they would be more relaxed taking their coffee and brandies at his palatial home. For her part, Sara, who had almost got to the point where she felt that she might have overdone her feigned indifference to Steed, agreed with alacrity. The bill signed, they proceeded out of the restaurant and waited patiently under the awning while the car jockey chased down St James's for a taxi. In spite of the fact that it was still only the latter part of April, the night air was pleasantly warm, the good weather perhaps a signal that high summer for the year would be one long sheet of rain.

As a cab drew up, a man turned the corner and saw Steed and his companion wavering in front of his unfocused eyes. Steed started to hand Sara into the cab and the man staggered across the pavement and touched Steed on the shoulder.

'Steed.'

He turned and looked into the unshaven face and bloodshot eyes of the drunk who had accosted him. The man was shabbily dressed, about forty-five, his face lined and ravaged by drink and nerves. In spite of the general air of decay, Steed noticed that he was sporting an old school tie. He had not yet completely fallen into the abyss of the wino. Even so, it took Steed more than a moment to recognise him—Freddy.

Steed's mind went back to the memorandum he had received

from 'Mother' on the day before their last case had started to burst wide open. It seemed like an age. The drunken Freddy peered up into his face and exhaled. His breath was heavy with stale liquor and it was all that Steed could do not to turn his head away.

Freddy said, 'I thought it was you. I knew I couldn't mistake that elegant shoulder.'

Steed looked at him with a mixture of compassion and understanding. He had been a good operative until his loss of nerve. Now he would never fully recover. It was sad that the Department had been forced to cut him off, sad but inevitable. He made sure that Sara was settled in the taxi, gave her a glance that said, 'give me a moment', then turned back.

'Hello, Freddy.'

Freddy's attention had been drawn to Sara and he leered into the taxi at her before replying, 'Well, John, you can still pick them—you always could . . . Hope you don't mind me stopping you like this. Just thought I'd say hello.'

'It's good to see you, Freddy.'

But the man was hardly listening. His mind was too fuddled by drink. 'I say, I hope I haven't embarrassed you, showing up like this. But I mean, well, I couldn't go by without saying hello, now could I?'

With that, he turned abruptly on his heel and, swaying from side to side so that his progress was a zig-zag rather than a straight line, he proceeded down the street, away from them.

Steed leaned into the cab. 'Listen, do you mind waiting a moment. I must speak to him. He was an old friend.'

Sara smiled, concealing her private thoughts and doubts that Steed should have such friends. 'Of course not.'

Steed walked quickly after Freddy. The man quickened his pace as he heard footsteps behind him, but he was weaving from side to side so much that it didn't take Steed long to catch up with him. He faced the drunken man and asked. 'Are you sure you're all right?'

'I'm fine—right as rain.'

'Then how are things—you have a job?'

Freddy blinked. 'Not at the moment, but there's one or two things coming up. Trouble is, I don't like sitting around—prefer something active.'

He looked as if he was going to cry. Steed said, 'If there's anything...'

The other man shook his head, then, 'How's the Department going—still managing to function all right without me—"Mother" managing as always?'

'Just about.'

The other man was suddenly serious and sober for a moment. One hand grasped Steed's lapel. 'Steed, old man. If they would give me another chance—I mean, if you could put in a word...'

His voice faded as he saw the look of compassion and sadness in Steed's eyes. He cleared his throat. 'No, of course not. Unfair to ask. It's been a long time. Too long.'

Steed opened his mouth to offer help, but the other man's pride had reasserted itself. 'Look, Steed, you'd better get back. You've kept that delicious lady waiting for far too long.'

'Freddy, can we at least drop you somewhere?'

'No thanks.' The answer was abrupt, snapped. Obviously, Freddy had fallen to such depths that he was too ashamed to let Steed know where he was living at present.

Steed's hand slipped inside his dinner jacket and he brought out his wallet.

'If you need a loan to tide you over...'

The other put a surprisingly firm hand in the centre of Steed's chest, pinioning the hand holding the wallet, so that he could not bring it right out but had to let it slip back down into the pocket. He made it very clear that he had not been after a handout.

'No thanks, Steed. Anything but that.'

Steed nodded. 'Well, Freddy, you know where I live. Come round any time. You're always welcome.'

The man managed a thin smile. 'With ladies like that around, I might well do that, old boy.'

The two men regarded each other in silence for a further moment. There was a lifetime of silent affection summed up in that look, then Freddy turned away and began to sway again down the street. Steed gazed after him, lost in thought, then abruptly, his mind snapped back into the present and he turned back to retrace his steps.

Sara was waiting patiently in the cab. 'Was he someone you worked with?'

Steed shook his head. To answer in the affirmative would be

a breach of security. 'Just an old friend I was at school with.'

'He seems to have fallen on hard times.'

Steed felt the sudden need to defend his old friend. 'Only for the moment, Sara, only for the moment.'

He slammed the door of the cab and they drove off, to Steed's apartment. But whatever he planned for the rest of the evening, it had been spoiled for him by seeing Freddy in such a state.

As for the drunken man, his spirits too were low as he walked through the almost deserted streets, making for his present unsalubrious lodgings. He spent the time thinking back on his work for the Department. Some men, like Steed, thrived on such work, their nerves responding to the calls of danger that were laid on them. Others, like Freddy, starting with the same intelligence and advantages, lacked that extra ingredient and were broken by their experiences. Once their nerve was gone, Freddy knew they were of no further use.

And yet, as he walked, he could still hope. Perhaps one day something would happen, he would find himself in a position to help the Department and to vindicate himself for his mistakes. The thought did not stay with him for long and, at last, he shrugged it aside, depressed by the reality of his situation. He had sunk too low ever to be rehabilitated and he knew it.

He did not know, however, that he was walking towards just such a dream as he had envisaged—that his moment of importance was close upon him.

It took him nearly an hour to get back to his present quarters. He had swayed down St James's, then across St James's Park and on to Birdcage Walk. From there he had crossed Parliament Square and the long open stretch of Westminster Bridge. There were still lights and traffic round Waterloo Station, but, beyond that again, were the mean little houses and the open scars of demolition of the Waterloo area. It was among these places that he had found a sort of sanctuary.

He turned into a street that consisted of derelict houses for part of the way, an already demolished area for the rest. The site had lain idle for over a year, affording him a comfortable sanctuary, as all demolition work had ceased with the bankruptcy of the high-flying property company who had acquired the site at the peak of the property boom. To Freddy, the collapse of the market had come as a blessing, so he had not been forced to find new accommodation. It was an ill wind that had worked in his favour, and he was not as gloomy about the economic situation as some.

Making sure that the whole of the ill-lit street was devoid of people, he ducked suddenly into a doorway, crossed the derelict building beyond and then went out through the non-existent back door and across an open space. His own quarters were beyond this. Down some broken steps in a half-demolished building was a cellar area that provided enough cover to shelter him from the weather, while the well-placed spaces afforded him a view over most of the area so that he would have good warning if anyone came on the site.

He flopped down on the old mattress that he had placed there, felt in his pocket and held up the bottle that he had secreted. It was still half full of whisky, enough for him to go to sleep on. He took a huge swig from the bottle and tried to put the meeting with Steed out of his mind.

This was a more difficult task than he thought and, as the bottle was consumed, he found that his fuddled mind kept going back to the sight of his old friend and colleague and the beautiful, mature woman he had been with. Steed had always been the lucky one, the one with the brains and the money. One day, Freddy promised himself, one day, he would show him, he would show them all.

The empty bottle slipped from his fingers on to the ground beside him as he drifted into a drunken sleep.

It was the noise of the Land-Rover that woke him to a dawn that was almost too full of light for him to open his eyes. Freddy sat up painfully. It was driving over rough ground near by, revving furiously as it went over the rubble. As it finally screamed into view, it stopped with a loud crash of gears.

Four men jumped from the vehicle—all of them wearing dungarees of a strange, drab colour—giving them the appearance of Commandos on manoeuvre—and this impression was reinforced by the fact that all were carrying high-powered rifles. As Freddy watched, his fuddled brain clearing at the sight of so much activity so early in the day and in such strange surroundings, they spread out and began to move away from him, as if they were searching for something. They moved very noisily, as if they wanted to use the noise to flush out whatever they were after.

As he watched from his covered position, a second Land-Rover screamed up and parked beside the first. There were only two men in the front of this one—but another man sat in the back. Freddy's interest in the scene became even more concentrated as he saw something familiar about the newcomer—who was obviously in charge.

Two of the first four men who had appeared hurried back to the second Land-Rover and nodded to the newcomer, as one of them said, 'He's definitely here, sir.'

'You're sure?'

The other man volunteered, 'I saw him, sir. He went into one of the old cellars over there, sir.'

'Right, Tayman.'

For a moment, Freddy had felt more than a frisson of fear at the thought that it might turn out to be himself for whom these well-armed strangers were looking. But as the man that the leader had identified as Tayman spoke, he had pointed to the piles of rubble that were the ghastly monument to the already demolished area on the far side of the wrecked site. He was able to return to the task of putting his alcohol-soaked mind together for long enough to remember the leader and what had been the circumstances when they had met. He knew that it had something to do with the Department and his job—but when and where?

As he watched, the man, who, unlike the others, was dressed in a comfortably tweedy suit, carefully removed a ring from his index finger and followed this up by taking a superb-looking gold watch on an expensive-looking gold strap off his wrist and placing them in one of his pockets.

From his pocket, he then took a pair of thin rubber gloves and, slowly and carefully pulled them over his hands. When he was ready, he gesticulated in the direction of where Tayman was sure their quarry, human or animal, had gone to earth. 'You two can cover the rear. I want the rest of the men to cover the front, to make sure he doesn't come out as you go in—right?'

'Right, sir.'

He stepped down from the vehicle and Freddy could now see that he was wearing long rubber boots, his tweed trousers tucked neatly into the top of them. He looked for all the world like a gentleman farmer out to inspect a cow barn. It was then that Freddy noticed that all the men were also wearing rubber boots and rubber gloves. The vision was getting curiouser and curiouser by the minute—and still there was something familiar about their leader. Freddy had now got enough ideas into his head to feel that the man either was, or had once been in charge of some government establishment—an establishment with a secret enough character so that Freddy had been sent down to advise security for the Department. As Freddy was now remembering, bit by bit, the man had very much resented the intrusion on what he regarded as his private domain, rather than a publicly-owned establishment.

The men moved quickly through the rubble until they reached the cellars for which they were aiming, Tayman in the lead. They reached the largest of these dips in the ground. At the bottom of some broken steps was an old door that stood ajar within the dust and rubble. Tayman pointed down excitedly.

'He went in there, sir.'

Turner went cautiously down the steps and put his eye to a crack in the door. After a moment, he turned and retraced his steps, nodding thanks to Tayman. He made a signal to the other men who stood back and cocked their weapons at the ready.

'I want him alive if possible, Simpson.'

The man nodded and went down the steps. He measured up the door with his eye, then stepped back, took a short run at it and crashed through in a flying dropkick. He hit the door with a dreadful crash and it fell open, propelling him through to the dangers beyond.

By this time, even Freddy had left his cover and had scrabbled his way over piles of rubble, to be able to look down on the strange scene. Simpson picked himself up and backed away from the door. The other men moved in closer and Freddy could now see that many of them had torches in their free hands. Like himself, they all peered forward into the stygian gloom of the cellar beyond the smashed door.

The leader took a torch from one of his men and went very

slowly down the steps to stand in the doorway. He switched on and swung the beam into the space beyond so that it cut through the darkness, illuminating parts of the deserted cellar like the single spotlight on the stage of a theatre.

The cellar was small and dark and at first the torchlight fell on just the dirt and rubble of the interior, revealing nothing as it swung from side to side in its search. Then, quite suddenly, something white flashed into the beam as it passed over and the man abruptly returned to it. Sitting in the light of the torch, trembling with almost mortal fear, was a small white guinea-pig.

For a second, Freddy thought he was in delirium tremens. Before he had time to recover fully from the sight in the torchlight, Tayman pushed past his master and shouted, 'There he is.'

As he ran forward, the other man made an effort to grab his shoulder and hold him back, but he missed his hold entirely.

'No. You mustn't frighten him.'

It was too late. Tayman ran forward, bent down and scooped up the tiny, white animal. He turned round, triumphantly cradling the tiny creature in his gloved hands.

'I told you, sir. I told you I saw him.'

One of the other men came down the steps holding a large box, the holes in the open top giving witness to the fact that it was for the use of the little animal. Tayman went forward to drop the creature in its trap, then, as he let go of it, he said, 'Damn.'

He held one of his hands. Even as he had dropped the helpless little creature in its box, it had managed to have some tiny revenge by biting his hand through the rubber of the glove.

The lid of the box was secured and the man carrying it moved back up the steps and over towards one of the Land-Rovers. The leader stayed by the door of the cellar and, as Tayman went past him, he stopped the other man.

'Show me your hand.'

Peering down from his circle position, Freddy watched the man pale and try almost physically to hang back. The older man stepped forward and, in spite of the younger one trying to dodge him, he grabbed the arm which Tayman thrust behind his back.

'I said I want to see your hand.' The words were barked out

by a man who was not used to being disobeyed.

Reluctantly, the man let his arm relax, then brought it in front of himself again, so that the other man was able to lift the hand and inspect the rubber glove on it. He found the tiniest of tears in the rubber, made by the animal's teeth and he lifted it with a finger of his own glove.

Tayman looked terrified at what the other man had discovered and tried to pull away. 'It's all right, sir.'

The other man shook his head. 'No, Tayman.'

Tayman began to tremble. From where Freddy was lying, he could not understand the reason for the man's sudden fear.

'Please, sir. It's all right—it just nipped the skin—didn't even draw blood.'

The other man let the hand drop. 'I'm sorry, Tayman.'

He turned from Tayman and walked slowly up the steps. The other man who had reported with Tayman on his arrival was standing at the top of the steps, his machine-gun at the ready.

'He's all yours, Simpson.'

Simpson nodded and started down the steps. Below, Tayman screamed out, 'No, sir. Please.'

He started up the steps to follow the leader, but Simpson pushed the gun barrel at his chest and forced him back down, so that he was flat against the door that Simpson had broken such a short time before. 'Please—Professor Turner—sir, Please.'

But the Professor was striding away in the direction of the Land-Rover, as if trying to put as much distance as possible between himself and the man he had ordered to be shot.

He froze as one shot rang out. He turned to the man who had carefully put the box containing the white guinea-pig in one of the Land-Rovers.

'It was the kindest way.'

He climbed slowly into the Land-Rover in which the box had been placed and the driver started the machine. As he drove off, Freddy tried to place the name and the face in his rag-bag of experiences and memories as he watched the further activity of the men who remained behind.

First they went back to their Land-Rover and, from the floor at the back, they produced a large plastic bag, of the kind that local council authorities give out for the storing of rubbish. They retraced their steps to the cellar where the dead body of Tayman lay and, with what appeared to be an exaggerated care to touch him with nothing other than their gloves, they loaded him into the sack and sealed it carefully before carrying it over to the Land-Rover and putting it in the back.

Even Freddy could see a reasonable explanation for this behaviour. If they wished to carry away the evidence of their crime, they would avoid getting blood on themselves or the seat of the vehicle. But the original reason that the man had been shot—that Freddy could not fathom.

The other Land-Rover started up and went slowly across the rubble back to the road. Soon even the sound of it had died away and the open area was quiet once more. It was barely six a.m. and nothing was yet stirring on these streets.

Freddy went back to his resting place, deep in thought. Professor Turner. He was sure that he remembered the name, but not sure where from. He was assailed by a sudden thought and ran back up into the derelict area. He climbed as quickly as his condition allowed up on one of the half-demolished buildings which was higher than the rest and his eyes roved the surrounding streets in an effort to spot one of the Land-Rovers. His luck was in. The second one to leave was proceeding down a shabby road towards the river and he smiled in satisfaction. The road only led to one place—a derelict part of the docks. He would have little trouble finding the Professor and his men again.

After his early-morning exertions, he felt tired and in need of a drink. He stumbled through his store of old bottles but could find none that contained enough liquid to swallow. Instead, he lay down to have a little sleep before continuing his investigations. There was a new excitement welling up in him.

When he had seen Steed the night before, he had no reason to suppose that his ruined life would change in any way—now he was not so sure. And this thought made the lack of a drink hurt less than it would normally have done.

Freddy was not the only person to have a disturbed night. Steed had finally decided to take Sara out to his house in the country, with the fulsome excuse that she might as well stay overnight in order to enjoy a good morning's riding. It was a reason that suited her book admirably and she had fallen in with it in short order, thus cancelling her ice-queen image in one moment.

The telephone call had come at four a.m. and Steed, fortunately waking first, had answered the phone. On the other end had been a highly excited Morgan. He had, with some difficulty, decoded Rostock's message and was all for reading it out over the phone. Steed had snapped, 'Be at my house at eight a.m.'

Sara had been disturbed by the phone and now turned to face him. 'What's the matter, darling?'

With little enthusiasm at that time of night Steed had proved that the only thing that was the matter with him was that he could not get enough of her. With an effort that had required years of training, he managed to stay awake after she had once more lapsed into an exhausted sleep and had then slipped from his bed and gone down to the study where he had placed two phone calls—one to Purdey, the other to Gambit. If he was to have so disturbed a night, he felt that there was no good reason why they should wake up fresh in the morning.

Purdey answered almost on the first ring, the sign of a clear conscience and a girl alone in her flat. With Gambit, it had taken a little longer and, from the giggling in the background, Steed guessed that the younger man was not confining himself to answering the phone.

The message to both of them was short and to the point. 'Something's broken on Rostock. Be at my country place at eight a.m.'

His troubles for the night were not yet over. At six o'clock, Sara, who seemed to be disgustingly fresh after her night's endeavours, woke him to suggest that they should both go riding. A moment of struggle and she had got the point home that (a) she was an evening lady and (b) she had meant on horseback. He had expressed his regrets.

'I have some people coming for breakfast.'

'Oh, how lovely. Who?'

He sighed. 'It's business.'

She pouted. It seemed absolutely ridiculous in a woman of

forty—or thirty-eight as she had admitted in a moment of abandon during the night. Still, her youthfulness of mind certainly kept her young in body. At length, and with a little physical persuasion, she agreed to go out riding and to rejoin Steed in mid-morning, when his meeting was sure to have broken up.

Promptly at eight o'clock, the door to Steed's study opened and Purdey marched in, looking as fresh as a daisy, as if she had just been on a week's holiday instead of one of the most dangerous assignments of her young life. She looked at Steed and said, 'Good God, what's the matter with you? You look like something the cat sicked up.'

He nodded a grim thanks at the compliment and, a moment later Morgan, who looked merely tired and Gambit, who looked rather like Steed felt, trooped in.

Steed showed them all to seats and Morgan thrust a copy of the decoded message at each of them. 'I've got down everything as far as he got before the line went dead.'

Steed said sharply, 'Could it have been power failure?'

Morgan shook his head. 'Not the way it happened. I haven't been able to raise him since—and his frequency signal has stopped transmitting—that went on for a while after he stopped.'

'For how long.'

'Oh, about three minutes.'

Steed nodded grimly. That was no power failure. Obviously the man had been forcibly removed from his set—whether by hand or with the aid of a bullet, it would amount to the same thing in the end in that part of the world. Later the set had been smashed or taken away.

In the meantime, Purdey and Gambit read out the message. 'Fat man arriving at 11.30 hours, Heathrow Airport. Wednesday.'

'That's today,' said Gambit helpfully but unnecessarily.

Purdey went on, 'To negotiate the purchase of Midas.'

She fell silent, for that was all there was to the message. Steed remained silent too and, at length, as the atmosphere in the room became oppressive, Purdey snapped, 'Care to comment on Midas, Steed?'

It was Morgan who answered, 'There's nothing code-named Midas on our books.'

Steed's brows were knitted in thought. 'No, there's no one named Midas—nothing of that name either.' He looked down at his copy of the message. 'Negotiate purchase—they're sending a man all this way to negotiate—but for what?'

Purdey chimed in, 'The only way to find that out is to find the man.'

Steed responded without a trace of irony, 'Gambit, get on the phone to the airport. Find out the origin of any flights coming in around eleven-thirty this morning.'

Gambit lifted the receiver of one of the phones on Steed's desk and dialled out at once. He seemed to carry the number in his head and Purdey noticed this, trying to think back to the last time she had ever seen him have to look up a number. As she did so, her gaze wandered round the almost aggressive masculinity of Steed's study, thence to the window that looked out over the side lawn and the rolling fields beyond, dappled by sunlight. She whistled. 'That's quite a case you have on your hands, Steed.'

The others all turned in the direction in which she had been looking, to see Sara, a short distance off in the fields cantering the horse she had chosen from the stables. Steed cleared his throat. 'Old friend of the family.' Even as he said it, he knew it wouldn't wash with Purdey, and also questioned why he had felt it necessary to make an excuse to her. As he watched Sara canter past, he put it out of his mind as just another manifestation of approaching middle age. It had been approaching for so long now, he hoped he would get fair warning when it arrived.

With an effort he brought his mind back to the subject at hand. 'Whatever else it is, this message is important. Rostock wouldn't have risked breaking silence—and possibly give his life—for a mere piece of international trivia.'

Gambit held up his hand. He had been talking quietly into the phone. Now he offered the receiver a brief thanks and replaced it. 'The eleven thirty flight that will arrive this morning is from Paris, Milan and—Peking.'

Even Morgan was alerted by that. Steed looked thoughtful, stood up and walked over to the window where he could observe Sara still putting the horse through its paces. After a long silence, he sighed, 'A pity—to have to go and look for a fat man on a lovely day like this.'

Purdey had the bad taste to snigger and Gambit groaned. He knew that they had been assigned for the airport job. Steed went on, 'I had something altogether thinner in mind.'

Purdey sighed, 'It's okay. We'll handle it.'

Steed turned on her. 'We'd better take our own cars.'

'We?'

Steed smiled. 'Well, I'm coming too. It's too important to miss.'

'But I thought . . .'

'Then you thought wrong.' Steed turned back to Morgan. 'Go and get some sleep. Then check the listening post tonight to see if Rostock has made contact again. Though, after what you've told me, I doubt it.'

He opened the window. 'Sara.'

She turned, and because she was beginning to get to know John Steed quite well, said, 'I know. You've got to go out and you don't know when you'll be back.'

'Quite right. I don't. Stay as long as you like. If I'm not back in a week, I'll call—promise.'

He blew her a kiss before she had time to open her mouth to argue, then turned back to the others. 'Right. Let's go and meet a fat man, shall we?'

As they came down the steps into Steed's immaculately kept gravel drive, he said to Purdey, 'Midas—he was a legendary king, wasn't he—ancient Greek or something?'

Purdey grinned. 'And everything he touched was turned to gold.'

Steed laughed. 'This could be quite fun.'

Chapter Eight

Professor Turner sat calmly as the gates that led into the derelict docks were opened and the two Land-Rovers passed inside. He waited in a side street for the other Land-Rover to rejoin him after its occupants had carried out their grizzly work of wrapping up Tayman's body. It was still too early for anyone to be about in this largely deserted neighbourhood, but, if the gates were opened and closed too often, they might be spotted. It was for this reason too, that there was a rota for using different entrances to the abandoned area.

The Land-Rovers drove past the old warehouses and round the detritus of the area's previous occupations. In the centre of the area, almost completely surrounded by the old, decaying buildings, was what had been the administrative block from where the whole complex had been run. It was for this that the Professor and his men were making.

As he drove into the yard that confronted them, he noticed that a gleaming car was waiting by the door, empty. He stepped down, the box containing the recaptured guinea-pig in his hands, and a guard approached.

'Mr Vann is here, sir. I've put him in reception.'

'Thank you.' He turned to the others. 'Dispose of Tayman, then go about your duties.'

He swept in through the main door of the building. If, on the outside, the place still gave the impression of having been left to crumble, inside this was quickly dissipated. The whole interior of the building had been decorated and prepared to be a home and laboratory, not only for the Professor and the object of his experiments, but for his men as well.

Mr Vann was waiting in a deep leather armchair in the hallway beyond the main doors. He stood as the Professor entered. 'Good morning, Professor. There has been a little contretemps, I understand.'

Pausing only to glare at the offending guard who had opened his mouth, the Professor said, 'Come through to the laboratory with me.'

Mr Vann fell in behind him, his immaculately cut suit in direct contrast with the Professor's tweeds and rubber boots and gloves. Vann was a tough-faced man of about thirty-five, his only affectation a drooping Zapata moustache.

Inside the laboratory, the Professor waited until the doors had closed and they were alone, then he held up the box. 'Here is our little truant.'

He placed the box on the table, opened a drawer and produced a pair of gauntlets made of heavy clear plastic. He drew these on over the rubber gloves he already wore, then opened the lid of the box with care—amused that Vann backed away down the room. He held up the tiny, inoffensive creature in the gauntlets and said, 'I had entirely overlooked his sheer voracity. He gnawed through the wood of his box and escaped us.'

Vann sighed. 'That could have been a bad mistake.'

'Yes, Mr Vann, it could indeed. But we have him back now.'

As he spoke, he opened a large cage and slipped the guinea-pig inside.

'He is the forerunner of an illustrious line. The Midas Prototype, so to speak.'

'Why Midas?'

Turner shut the door of the cage, making sure that it was fastened securely, then he turned, smiling to the other man. 'Have I not discovered the way to turn dross into gold?'

He walked to the door of the laboratory and ushered the other man out. A little way down the corridor was Turner's own private room and he opened the door, allowing the other man to precede him inside. Vann had never been in the sanctum on his previous visits and what met his eyes made him gasp in admiration and wonder.

The room was entirely unexpected after the starkness and functionalism of the laboratory. The whole room gleamed golden—everything possible was fashioned from the metal itself. The room was decorated with a number of solid gold objects. Glass panes hung down the walls, adorned with hundreds of golden sovereigns. The room was a total reflection of the Professor's well-known obsession with the metal.

'As you can see, gold is very important to me.'

Vann could only nod dumbly at the sight before him and Turner went on, 'Oh, there are those who prefer platinum or silver. I find such metals cold and totally without character. No, give me gold every time, Mr Vann. Lots of gold. It makes one feel so—so sunny, don't you think?'

Privately, Vann thought the word for which the Professor was searching was rich, but he suppressed the inclination to say so. Instead, he cleared his throat with a polite impatience and asked, 'When do I meet Midas?'

'Patience, Mr Vann. Patience.' Turner moved around the room, polishing a piece of metal here, an object there. He had stripped off the gauntlets and the rubber gloves below them and had let them fall into a golden basket near the door. Now his hands caressed his possessions as if they had a life of their own.

Vann snapped, 'You have had my offer for weeks. All the time you have counselled patience—now time is short. I need his services.'

The Professor shook his head. 'Mr Vann, as you know— Midas—or rather the secret of Midas will go to the highest bidder—and you are not the only potential buyer.' He paused and glanced at the beautiful gold watch which he pulled from the pocket in which he had placed it during the hunt for the guinea-pig and replaced it on his wrist. 'Quite soon, you will have a rival to bid against.'

'If he turns up.'

Turner had his back to Vann. Now he stiffened and turned quickly, but the other man was smiling blandly.

'Is that a threat, Mr Vann?'

Vann shrugged. 'Of course not, Professor. I do not even know who my rival is to be. It is just that I have waited so long that I begin to think that he might be a figment of your imagination—a character of fiction, drawn in order to make my bid high and to keep the price up.'

The Professor relaxed. 'By this afternoon, I am hopeful that you will discover that he is very much alive—perhaps even larger than life.'

'He is coming today, then?' Vann kept his face expressionless as he asked the question. Already, the information that his rival was due to arrive on a flight at eleven-thirty that morning had been brought to him through the spy network that his position in his own country and in Britain caused him to maintain. Already he had taken steps to try to ensure that his bid alone would stand for what he needed.

'Yes,' said the Professor. 'He is coming at last today.'

Freddy woke suddenly, jerked into wakefulness. His mouth was very dry and thick. He glanced round, but there seemed nothing but a sea of empty bottles round him. As he groped, looking for one that might contain some liquid fire with which he might prepare himself to face the day, the memory of his previous awakening came back to him. It passed through his mind like a series of photo impressions. The two Land-Rovers arriving—the men with their machine-guns. The breaking into the cellar—the man who had come out in triumph with the guinea-pig. The bite he had received. The killing and the men carrying him away in the plastic sheeting. But above all, he remembered Professor Turner. The Professor had been one of the more eccentric workers at the Pilton Down germ-warfare establishment. His work was good and he was as normal as any of them, but he had been obsessed by gold. Every penny he could make went on the buying of gold objects, on the decoration of his quarters in gold and with gold.

Freddy remembered going down over a security scare and

finding Turner's methods of guarding his gold were almost as elaborate as the security methods for the whole establishment.

But that had all been a long time ago. Pilton had been closed for nearly six years. Professor Turner, so he had heard, had gone to work abroad. There had been a dreadful row, he remembered, because he had not been able to take his gold objects with him— they had had to be left in a vault to await his return. Well, now it seemed the Professor had returned and with a vengeance.

Freddy managed to get to his feet and stay on them. He was determined that he would not let the opportunity of his vantage point of that morning slip through his fingers. There was a mystery here. A murder at least, but his instincts told him that there was a lot more—perhaps even enough to get the Department to take him back again.

This thought steadied the shell of a man. He set off in the direction that he had seen Turner and his men go—the direction of the old docks.

In the end, Purdey had travelled to the airport with Steed in his car, Gambit following in his own. When they had arrived, Gambit had parked his machine on the front of the arrivals building, Steed in a special area at one side. Now, while Gambit kept his position by the repetitious flashing of his special pass to busy-body police and traffic wardens who came up to him, John Steed and Purdey moved into the main arrival hall.

The business of the day was in full swing and a large crowd moved through the concourse. Over their heads a muffled tannoy announced the arrivals and departures of the aeroplanes.

Steed went to the news-stand and purchased a copy of the day's *Times*. There was little news of an exciting nature. There was pressure on the pound, the government were in trouble, the opposition was in disarray. Things were much as usual. A picture of a dazzling woman on the front page drew Steed's attention for a moment. It was accompanied by a caption announcing that the Princess had arrived, accompanied by her Prime Minister, for the opening of the exhibition of Golden Antiques from her country. Steed turned to the sports page, but found nothing to interest him there. His horses never seemed to come up.

As Steed went to the news-stand and then to a good spot from where he would be able to watch all the arrivals come through from customs control, Purdey had gone to the enquiry desk to check up on the plane. Now she returned.

'Our quarry should be in the next load through. That was the last plane to come in.'

Steed did not bother to lower the paper, and she asked, 'Can I have the crossword?'

Now he lowered the paper long enough to give her a withering look. 'My dear, in spite of the advance of Women's Rights and the liberation movement there are still some things that are sacred to an Englishman—and one of them is his copy of *The Times*. If you are so anxious to pit your wits against the greatest crossword brains in the world, then I suggest you get your own.'

He raised the paper again and Purdey smiled. There were some things about Steed you could always rely on. A moment later there was a bustle at the customs door and the first passengers off the eleven-thirty arrival began to filter through.

Steed folded his paper and watched carefully as they did so. There was a catholic assortment in the first batch, but none that could actually be described as fat. Purdey swore. 'Damn. He should be among this lot.'

A moment later, he emerged unmistakably through the doorway. When Rostock had sent a message about a fat man, his description had been precise.

The man who came through the doorway and blinked about him, as if he expected to be met, was enormous. His face was that of a bluff Englishman, apart from a slight Mongol slant round the eyes. From his cheerful face downwards he opened up like one of those toys which cannot be knocked over. Even his legs seemed to bulge as he waddled forward. Steed thought that he was the fattest man he had ever seen.

Purdey said excitedly, 'That has to be him.'

A moment later Steed had placed the features. The man who stood before him had always been big—but never as obese as this. He looked as if he had flown in for a competition to find the fattest man in the world. Steed said slowly, 'But that's an old friend—Hong Kong Harry. I hardly recognised him for a moment—he's put on so much weight.'

Steed and Purdey were not the only people in the arrivals area who were on the lookout for Hong Kong Harry. As soon as the man had appeared in the doorway, another man, dressed in the livery of a chauffeur and carrying a card had moved forward. He held up the card as he approached the fat man and, glancing at it, Purdey was able to read that scrawled on it were the simple words: 'Mr Smith.'

As he approached Harry, the man was holding the card in one hand at waist level. As Steed and Purdey watched, a few people passing between them and the fat man, there came a noise, almost unidentifiable above the din. A hole appeared in the card, then the smile disappeared from the fat man's face as he stopped dead, grunted, clutched his ample belly and began to stagger to his knees.

In the same instant the chauffeur threw the card to one side and Purdey got a brief glimpse of a gun with a silencer. It disappeared into the man's pocket as he turned and made off quickly through the unsuspecting crowd. Apart from Steed and Purdey no one around had yet noticed that anything was wrong. It had all been done so quickly and smoothly that even they were partially mesmerised and rooted to the spot.

They turned their eyes back to the object of the surprise attack. Harry was still moving forward, staggering and falling. He was clutching his belly and, from the hole the bullet had made, streaming between his fingers came—not blood—but a stream of glittering gold dust. The sight of it galvanised Steed into action. 'Purdey—get him.'

The order triggered her off and she started across the concourse in pursuit of the fleeing assassin. Steed leaped the barrier and was the first person at Hong Kong Harry's side as he finally fell. His hand went down to join the other man's and verify that it was gold dust that was pouring out.

Seeing a man leap the customs-area barrier, the police were quickly on the scene. Steed's hand dived into his pocket as they came down on him and he flashed his pass. 'Keep this area clear—don't let anyone near us.'

In the face of authority, the policeman asked no questions but set about obeying his orders. An area was cleared round the fallen man, an area that allowed for the gold dust not to be dissipated or blown away.

Outside the building, Gambit was seeing off yet another traffic warden, this time a man who was obviously frustrated that he could not put a ticket on Gambit's car and see him off. He was busy out-facing the official when his attention was drawn to the doors as a man in chauffeur's uniform burst through them, ran for the car to which the snubbed warden was also making, pushed the man to the ground, jumped in and roared away.

A moment later, Gambit heard his name called and turned to see Purdey running through the doors. In an instant he had jumped in his car and was revving up. Purdey jumped into the passenger seat of the open machine without opening the door. As they zoomed away and, before she had time to give any instructions, he grinned and said, 'The chauffeur in the black car—right?'

'How did you know?'

'That's my secret—what happened?'

Purdey shook her head. 'You're never going to believe this, but he just shot the fat man.'

'Dead?'

'I don't think so—Steed's with him. But he's lost an awful lot of gold dust.'

'Gold dust?' In his surprise, Gambit almost lost control of the car for a moment. There were traffic lights coming up and they were changing to yellow. He put his foot on the accelerator and skidded through before the other cars who were now signalled as clear moved forward.

Purdey laughed. 'It seems that our fat man was known to Steed—and wasn't so fat as we thought he was. From the look of it, he was carrying an awful lot of gold dust round with him.'

'That would explain the "Midas" in the message—wouldn't it?'

But Purdey was still frowning in concentration and not because Gambit was driving faster and more recklessly than the car he was in had ever been designed for.

'I don't think so.'

'But the man was carrying gold dust—that's the link, surely?'

'What happened to your education?—Midas was an ancient king who had a spell cast on him—so that everything he touched

124

turned to gold—I don't think that's quite the same thing.'

Gambit shrugged, sending the car into a minor skid. He straightened it up. Now he could see his quarry on the fast road ahead of him. The man was going at top speed and it would take a little time to catch up with him. He decided to concentrate on this and leave the puzzle to Purdey—after all, he knew that she could do *The Times* crossword in ten minutes, five minutes faster than he could—and even he was able to beat Steed by a good while.

He drove silently until they reached London and were plunging through the narrow streets towards the river. Then Purdey, whose mind had been exercising itself on the puzzle, laughed.

'My God, all that gold dust pouring down.'

Gambit took a corner broadside, gaining a precious second on the fleeing man, then straightened up. 'It's a difficult way to carry gold—gold dust. Why not Kruger-rands?'

'But it made a dramatic sight. It reminded me of that old Humphrey Bogart movie— you know, the one Walter Huston directed.'

'The treasure of the Sierra Madre.'

As he spoke the car came round a corner and went straight into an oil slick that lay across the road. Gambit slammed on his brakes as he went into it and the car spun round twice as it went through it. He had the dubious satisfaction, during the spin, of catching sight of the fleeing car straightening up a little way ahead—doubtless having its own trouble with the slick.

'Walter Huston didn't direct that—it was his son, John Huston.'

As he spoke, he skidded round another corner, saw a badly-parked car slewed round in the road, the driver pale at the wheel where he had been narrowly missed by the chauffeur. He had stalled and was staring with shock as Gambit came round the corner at him.

Gambit spun the wheel and mounted the pavement. The car passed narrowly between a lamp-post and the wall before he was able to regain the road. 'You know something—this bird can certainly drive. He's got a good chance of getting away.'

Another corner came up and Gambit took a chance, cutting

right across the pavement at the corner to make up for lost time. Purdey was thoughtful. 'You know, I think for once you're right.'

'Of course, I flaming am—did you see the way he handled that last corner. He's bloody good.'

'I wasn't talking about that. I mean about John Huston. He did direct it.'

Round the next corner the road opened up into a market area. As they came round, they were in time to see the car they were pursuing skid round the edge of a great pile of old boxes that had been swept together for some mythical garbage collection after the last day of the market. Gambit had no time to take evasive action, so he careered through the boxes and hoped for the best. As the boxes crashed all round them and Gambit fought to retain control of the car, Purdey sucked her teeth and said thoughtfully, 'Walter Huston played one of the leads—didn't he?'

Gambit glanced at her only long enough to give visual expression to what she might do with not only herself but Walter Huston, John Huston, Humphrey Bogart and the treasure of the Sierra Madre itself, before accelerating up in pursuit once more. Purdey glanced at her watch. It showed that it was half-past twelve and she was beginning to feel hungry.

In the golden room, Professor Turner was glancing at the beautiful gold watch on his wrist. It, too, said that the time was half-past twelve. He frowned as Mr Vann said softly, 'You see—he isn't going to turn up.'

Turner watched him with a baleful glare as he moved around the room. He could hardly suppress a shudder as he watched the exquisitely dressed young man touching his precious golden possessions.

Vann finished his round of the room and faced the Professor across the desk. 'Gold—I can well understand your obsession with the metal, Professor. I can feel it too. The mere thought of this pure golden metal, yellow and gleaming, can set a man's pulse racing.'

Turner had shut his eyes at the softness of the other man's voice. He could almost feel gold running over him, molten yet cool, covering him, the ultimate sensuous experience.

'Yes...Yes.'

Vann went on, breathing the words as he leaned closer to the other man—literally seducing him.

'To touch it—to feel it—just to own such things. With some men it is paintings—or women—the emotion is the same...'

'Yes...Yes...'

'It tightens the throat—it clouds the vision—it is Valhalla, the home of the Gods...'

Turner rose, his eyes still closed. 'Yes...Yes...'

Vann thumped the desk. 'I feel the same.'

The spell was broken. Turner opened his eyes and blinked quickly. 'About gold.'

Vann shook his head. 'No—not gold. About power—absolute power.'

During the silence this produced in Professor Turner, Vann reached into his inside pocket and produced a pamphlet which he laid on the desk. 'We can do business. Here is my offer.'

Turner did not glance down at the pamphlet, he pushed it away with an unseeing hand. 'We must wait. The other bidder has not yet arrived.'

Vann leaned forward, grabbed the pamphlet and forced it into the other man's hand, before he forced that same hand up to the Professor's face. 'Every item in there shall be yours.'

Slowly, against his will, Professor Turner looked at the glossy pamphlet that had been thrust at him. It was a brochure for an exhibition that was to open in London in a few days time—an exhibition of Gold Antiquities. Greedily, he leafed through it. Here were all the great treasures of the Incas and Aztecs—the great sunbursts, the crowns, the jewelery and artifacts that had been collected from all over the world—and all of it was gold.

Turner held his free hand out to the man in front of him. 'You shall meet Midas.'

He strode over to the door and opened it, beckoning Vann to follow him. This time they went back through the laboratory and out the other side. As they walked through the laboratory, Vann glanced at the live animals in their cages and the strange scientific equipment. He saw again the guinea-pig lying in the cage in which it had been put after its recapture. On the far side of the laboratory was a locked door. The Professor took a key from a chain in his trouser pocket and unlocked it. They went through into the inner, private and secret area and the door closed behind them.

On the old fire escape on the outside of the building, unsteady now and liable to sudden movements that frightened the man balanced on it, Freddy crouched down and waited until the laboratory was empty, then he stood again and went back to work on the window he had been trying to open. He was a bit rusty in his technique. That, combined with the shaking of his hands from the lack of a drink, was making it hard work. At last, the sash gave and he was able to slide it up and climb into the room.

He went to the door through which the men had left and tried the handle cautiously, but it had relocked automatically. He glanced round the room at the animals in their cages and the strange equipment but, after a few minutes, he could see that the paraphernalia in here would tell him nothing, so he crept to the door of the laboratory and opened it cautiously. He had not forgotten the guards with their machineguns—nor what they had done to one of their number, never mind a stranger. The corridor was empty and, after waiting a while, he went out into it and along to the first door.

This he opened as cautiously as he had opened the door to the corridor and, as soon as he was sure the room was empty, he opened it the whole way and stood on the threshold. His heart was in his mouth, beating loudly, echoing through his head. His mouth was dry and there was a film of sweat all over his face.

On the far side of the room he saw the most important thing he was looking for, a table on which stood three decanters, each of crystal but with a golden stopper. He homed in on them, saw which one was filled with the golden glow of Scotch whisky— Freddy's God now, as much as gold was the Professor's, then looked round briefly for a glass. He saw none and, impatiently, he removed the stopper and took a swig from the decanter. Two more swigs and his hands had stopped shaking, the sweat of fear and need gone from his forehead. Now he was able to look round and take in more easily the contents of the room. He whistled with amazement at the gold statuary and the coins on their glass panes. Then he moved over to the desk and glanced at the papers on top of it. The pamphlet for the Antiquities exhibition, he pushed to one side—it meant nothing to him. There were no drawers to the desk, so his searching was soon over. He was no further ahead with his investigations. He went back to the decanters and took another swig of Scotch. Then he was ready to go back to the laboratory and try a more thorough search.

On the other side of the door on the far side of the laboratory, Vann had been ushered into the sanctum sanctorum of Professor Turner's research establishment. He found himself in a corridor that was long and bare save for—at three equal intervals down it—a kind of hoop-shaped device hanging from the ceiling.

Turner led the man down the corridor and, as they passed under the first of these hoops, Vann jumped back as a fine aerosol spray came down on them. The Professor had walked on, taking no notice of the spray. He turned back and beckoned the other man on with a look of impatience.

'Please come on. It is just a necessary precaution.'

Vann pulled himself together and walked through the spray that came down as he walked under the hoop. The same thing happened going under the other two hoops, except that the spray emitted a different scent.

At the end of the corridor was another door. Turner stopped and tapped on it quietly. 'Midas.'

A lock was snapped back and the door at the end of the corridor began to open.

The chase through the narrowing streets towards the old docks of London was still going on, but the odds on the man escaping from Gambit and his lovely passenger were getting shorter by the moment. At length, after twisting and turning through the narrow streets, the chauffeur skidded through one of the badly closed gateways into the docks themselves, smashing the rusting gates apart with the force of his speed.

Once inside the docks, the man realised that he would need more than speed and driving skill to get away. He skidded round the side of an old warehouse, then braked abruptly. He flung open the car door as it came to a halt, then, with the engine still running, he leaned back inside and put the automatic gear-shift into reverse, before darting into the cover of the warehouse and running through to find safer cover.

The car began to move backwards, gaining speed. Gambit crashed over the broken dock gates in pursuit. He swung the car round the side of the warehouse, then both he and Purdey reacted in horror as they saw the other car speeding backwards towards them.

Gambit swung the wheel and skidded towards the wall of the warehouse. Faster than the eye could see the other car sped past him, missing them by inches. As for his own, it stalled to a halt a hairsbreadth away from the warehouse wall. As he and Purdey jumped down, they were in time to see the abandoned car hit the wall of another warehouse, careen off in a shower of sparks, before bursting into flames.

Gambit started forward, but Purdey snapped, 'Don't bother. He wasn't in it.'

Instead she turned and ran into the warehouse. Gambit followed. She was just inside and signalled him to halt. They stood in momentary silence, not moving, not breathing. In the far distance they could both hear footsteps. As soon as Purdey had located the direction from which they came, she pointed silently, then they both ran forward. At the far end of the warehouse were two exits. They paused, glanced at one another, gave a nod that betokened the complete understanding between them in such moments of crisis, then each took a different doorway, running forward in the hope that they might enflank and encircle the running feet.

The man continued his run, though he could now hear pursuing footsteps and was beginning to panic. Gambit, coming through the doorway he had chosen, found the way ahead of him clear and raced forward. Purdey, on the other hand, soon found her way completely blocked down a narrow passage between buildings by piles of packing crates. She leaped up on them and kept going. There were big gaps between them and leaping over the gaps slowed her down, but, from her position high up, she was able to anticipate the direction of the chase.

The fleeing man found the entrance to another warehouse and dived in. He found himself in an open space and began to run pell-mell across it to the open door at the far end.

He was half way across when he heard a sound behind him and turned. Gambit stood in the open doorway. The man went down on one knee and the gun with the silencer he had used to shoot the fat man flashed into his hand. As he fired, Gambit hit the concrete floor and rolled over.

The man turned and recommenced his run. By the time Gambit had picked himself up he had disappeared through the open door at the far end. Gambit crossed the open space and, as he came through the second doorway, a bullet smacked into the wall near his head. Once more he hit the deck. The running man turned away again and ducked between two old buildings.

Meanwhile, Purdey had run right past the second warehouse on the far side. She was back on the ground again and she stopped, waiting for a sound that would tell her what direction the chase had taken. She heard the distant sound of feet on metal and closed her eyes, the better to be able to judge the direction. Satisfied she had a mental fix on it, she turned and ran towards the noise.

The fleeing man had entered one of the old warehouses that he had dodged between and had found a catwalk. He had run up the iron steps and was now ducking along the catwalk, the cover it provided being negated by the sound of his footsteps made on the metal. There was a door ahead—a closed door this time. He made for it, then ducked as he reached it. Neither of his pursuers were yet in the same building and he had time to open the door cautiously.

Beyond the door was a narrow platform that led to iron steps that went down to the deck area below. The man moved cautiously out on to the platform, crouching low, his gun at the ready.

All he had to do was wait for his pursuer. The trap was perfect. In the warehouse below, he could hear Gambit's footsteps as, now moving cautiously, he came through the building.

The man looked back through the doorway into the building. He could see his pursuer in the area below.

Purdey came across the space between two buildings towards the building where she had heard the noise. She was at the far end of the warehouse from the waiting man. Here too, there was a staircase leading towards a platform and a doorway. Silently, she went up to the platform and opened the door slowly, ducking as she did so. She only needed to open it a crack. There, at the far end of the catwalk that stretched the length of the warehouse, silhouetted in the open doorway at the far end, was the crouching man, his gun at the ready. He was looking down into the warehouse, taking no notice of the opening door at Purdey's end. She carefully gauged the distance. Now all she could pray for was the time as she heard Gambit blundering down below.

She slid through the door and let it close behind her. The darkness behind her would make her more difficult to see if the man glanced up. She lifted herself on to her points. Below her she could see Gambit stepping closer and closer into danger. The man lifted his gun. He had to be careful, accurate—he had not got many shots left.

Purdey began to dance along the catwalk on her points. When she judged that she was close enough she prepared to go into her spin. Gambit was right below, the man poised, ready to fire. She had to move now, even if the distance was too great.

With a cry to get the man's attention, she spun forward. She had judged the distance just right. The man's gun came up, but he was a split second too late. Her foot caught him under the chin and, with a scream, he fell back, hit the platform, then spun over and crashed down to the ground.

Below, Gambit spun round and looked up. Purdey smiled down at him. 'He's closer to you.'

Gambit was galvanised into action. He ran out of the warehouse and stopped short when he saw the body. Purdey came down the steps and joined him. He shook his head. 'Purdey, we wanted him alive.'

She shrugged. 'It was a difficult choice, Gambit. Him or you.'

He bowed to her with mock solemnity. 'Thank you for making the right decision.'

Purdey laughed. 'If it's going to make you big-headed, I'll begin to regret it."

There wasn't time for him to glare, so he knelt down and began to go through the man's pockets. There was the usual collection of keys and small change. There was a wallet with a few notes in it, but no other identification. He could find no driver's licence or any other identification. He looked at the man's features. They were European, except for a slight hint of a slant around the eyes.

There was something sticking out of the man's top pocket and Gambit slid it out. It was an invitation—an invitation to a party that night at a country address. Gambit slid it into his pocket. He looked up at Purdey who was checking the number on the man's gun. It had been filed off.

'There's nothing more we can do here,' he said. 'Let's leave it for the police.'

'We'd better see what Steed's got.'

They left the gun on the body, then went back to Gambit's stalled car. When they saw how close they had been to the wall, they realised how nearly they had hit it and burst into flames like the other car had.

Purdey leaned in, opened the glove compartment and pressed a button inside. At once a special aerial sprouted on the front of the dashboard. Purdey picked up a transmission mike from the glove compartment, waited until the light on it glowed red, then pressed and spoke.

'Hello, Steed.'

'Where are you?'

'We're at the docks.'

'Did you get the man?'

'Too well, I'm afraid. He's dead.'

She listened while Steed tutt-tutted down the line. 'Really, Purdey, we have to curb your enthusiasm. I'll see you at my house in an hour—okay?'

'Okay.'

As they drove through the shattered remains of the gate, Gambit said, 'Can you make sense of any of this?'

'I can't see the wood for the trees—and I don't know where to start looking,' Purdey replied.

As she spoke, she did not glance back at the area from which they had come. On the other side of the same docks area was

Professor Turner's secret headquarters. Inside it was a man,
disowned by the Department, loved by not even himself, who
was trying to find the answers to the questions that Purdey,
Gambit and even Steed himself had not yet asked.

Chapter Nine

With the abrupt departure of Purdey and Gambit from the arrivals building at London Airport, only Steed stood between the recumbent form of Hong Kong Harry and the full majesty of the law. Steed's first major task was to turn Harry over on his back, so that no further gold dust would pour away from the hole made in the bag of it by the would-be assassin. The shock of having a gun fired at him at almost point-blank range had caused Harry to faint away—that being the cause of his fall—and it was a hard and heavy job to turn him over.

Steed then demanded of the policemen who crowded round, a dustpan and brush, a plastic bag and a luggage trolley—in that order.

After some unspoken argument, the men were stared down and went about their tasks. Other men held back the large crowd that was collecting. Steed leaned over the stricken man so that he hid his head from view. As soon as Harry's eyelids flickered open, Steed beamed down at him and whispered, 'Keep your eyes shut, Harry. You're supposed to be shot. We've got to get you out of here.'

The man beamed up at him. 'Thanks, John.' Then he shut his eyes and feigned unconsciousness.

The dustpan and brush duly arrived and Stood took them himself, and carefully swept up all the gold dust into the pan, making sure that not a grain was left on the ground. He made one of the policemen hold open the plastic bag so that he could pour the gold in. He sealed the bag and handed it over.

'Hold that and bring it with you when we go to my car.' He turned to some of the other policemen. 'I need volunteers.'

With doubtful looks at each other, all of them stepped forward. Steed picked the four toughest looking. 'Now, we've got to get this man on to that trolley.'

A policeman protested. 'But he's a wounded man.'

Steed's argument was unanswerable. 'I don't mind.'

In silence they helped load Harry on to the trolley in such a way that no more of the gold poured away. Then, accompanied by the policeman holding the plastic bag, he preceded the police-powered trolley out of the building, past the gaping crowds to his car. The police had more trouble putting Harry flat on the back seat of the car than they had had in any of the other manoeuvres. This done, Steed climbed into the driver's seat, thanked all and sundry and drove off. He was gone before one of the policemen asked who he was. There were a lot of red faces in the station that night, before the word came through to compliment them on their initiative—from the highest level.

On the open road to Steed's house, he said to the inert form in the back seat, 'It's all right for you to come round now, Harry, but don't sit up. I don't want gold dust all over the car.'

'Thanks, John.'

It was only as they walked up the steps of his house that Steed remembered he had abandoned Sara. He had no need to worry. There was a note stuck to the front door by a carving knife saying that she was walking to the station to catch the train to London. From the depth that the knife had been driven into the door, Steed suspected that she would not be interrupting them— ever again.

He led Harry into the study and sat him down carefully on a low chair. The fat man stripped off his jacket, revealing the fact that he was a great deal thinner than he had looked. Inside the voluminous coat he was draped all round with large bags of gold dust. Steed, with his help, began to take them all carefully from round his body. There was only a minute bruise on Harry's chest where the bullet from the silenced gun had hit the bag of gold dust. Steed laughed. 'You're barely scratched, Harry. These acted like sandbags—except that it isn't sand.'

Harry smiled as he rocked to and fro. 'I really appreciate this, Steed, you know that.'

'I wouldn't thank me too soon.'

'How do you mean, Steed? I really appreciate what you've done—whisking me away from the airport—no hassle—no fuss.'

'No questions?'

Harry's face lost its habitual good humour. 'No questions. Mind you, Steed, if you're ever in my neck of the woods and you're lying in a pool of your own blood I'd be glad to do the same for you.'

'Like the time you came along and tried to stamp on my neck?'

Harry blushed and waved his stubby arms apologetically. 'Steed. You know I wouldn't do a thing like that.'

He tried vainly to meet Steed's eye. It had happened in Hong Kong almost ten years before. They were old friends in the espionage and intelligence business but on that occasion they had found themselves on opposite sides of the fence. Steed had come as close to death at Harry's hands as he had ever done.

Harry said at last, 'Not unless I was well paid.'

Steed became serious. 'What's this about, Harry?'

All the gold bags were off him now. He was still a big man but the fat was an illusion. Hong Kong Harry was two hundred and fifty pounds of bone and muscle. He stood up and began to walk up and down, a sure sign that he was puzzled and alarmed. 'Oh, come on, Steed. How would I know? I was just hired as courier for that gold.'

'Just a courier for at least half a million pounds in gold?'

'Three quarters of a million actually—but that's all I know, honest injun.'

Steed said quietly, 'Come off it, Harry.'

'I swear it—on my mother's grave.'

'Harry, you couldn't even find your mother's grave. You sold it for development years ago.'

'Just because I'm a public-spirited citizen. Hong Kong's a small place—land's at a premium. She'd had use of it for a good long time. It was only right, Steed.'

Steed snapped, 'Midas.'

Harry stopped in mid-flow as if he had suddenly been frozen to the spot. He recovered quickly, but the slip had been there. Steed tried again. 'Midas—What does it mean, Harry?'

Harry sat down and spread his arms wide. It was a sign that he was really going to tell the truth. 'Something big, Steed. And that really is all I know. Something that's worth at least three quarters of a million pounds in gold.'

'You have nothing more than that?'

'You may not believe it, Steed. But that's the truth.'

In the disguised building in the docks, Freddy was also finding some truths of his own. He was going through every drawer in the laboratory, one at a time, searching through all the papers, looking for something that would provide the key to what was going on. There were various papers on disease-carrying and immunisation practices, but he couldn't make head or tail of the technical jargon in these so he ignored them.

Suddenly he heard sounds in the corridor that lay beyond the locked door at the end of the laboratory. They were almost at the door and he knew he would not have time to slip out into the corridor to find a hiding place. In the corner of the room stood a large cupboard. He went quickly over to it and opened the door, to find himself in luck. Apart from a few pairs of boots, the cupboard was bare. He got inside and closed the door, leaving only the slightest of cracks to allow him to see and hear what was going on.

The door at the far end of the laboratory opened and Professor Turner came through, accompanied by the well-dressed man who had been with him before, and whom Freddy had seen through the window when he had been crouched on the fire escape waiting for his chance to get into the building.

Once they were inside the laboratory and the door was closed again, the Professor turned to his companion. 'Well, Mr Vann—you are impressed by what you have seen, I trust?'

'Perhaps.'

'Only perhaps?'

'I have seen Midas, that is true. I have listened to your theories—but, in practical terms—I am going to need something more concrete than that, Professor.'

Turner nodded and invited the other man to come with him, back to his own room. They passed out of Freddy's sight and hearing as the door of the laboratory closed on them. Freddy came cautiously out of his cupboard and tip-toed over to the door, but he could hear nothing. They had moved away from it and along to the Professor's room of gold. Freddy licked his lips as he remembered the room—and the decanter of whisky with its gold top. He would rather be in there than in the laboratory, then he thought: well, you can't have everything when you are back on the job and he had at least the thought that he was back to sustain him. He set about looking through the laboratory once more—it was so important to find the answers—to find out who Midas was—or what.

In Turner's room the Professor had gone to his desk and had taken a piece of pasteboard up from it. He handed it to Vann. It was an invitation to a party—a similar one to the invitation that Gambit had found on the dead man—and Vann was puzzled by it.

'A party? I don't understand?'

'Your competitors—the men who did not turn up—they were as sceptical as you, Mr Vann—they demanded a demonstration—and I had arranged one—you had might as well attend it instead.'

Vann smiled—a smile that was returned by the Professor. 'I always enjoy a good party.'

Gambit and Purdey arrived at Steed's house within the hour they had been given. Gambit had driven a lot less fast on the way to Steed's house and had been forced to endure a stream of criticism on his driving technique from Purdey.

They had both been amused to find the kitchen knife stuck in the front door, even though Steed had torn the note off it. They went straight through to the study and found Steed calmly

139

drinking with the victim of the airport shoot-out. Steed said, 'Hong Kong Harry this is Purdey and Gambit, my two trusty helpers.'

The fat man smiled. 'The late Hong Kong Harry, I believe they thought from the looks on their faces.'

Steed clapped his hands together. 'Well, that takes care of the protocol—what did you find out?'

'Unfortunately, Purdey had done her party trick before we had a chance to talk, but I found this on him,' said Gambit.

He took the piece of pasteboard from his pocket and put it on the desk in front of Steed.

'That's quite close by. I think you ought to attend.'

'Right.'

Steed turned to Purdey, 'What actually happened to the real owner of this invitation?'

Purdey was at a loss. 'Well—er—he sort of fell for me.'

Gambit added, 'From a great height.'

Steed was thoughtful. 'Hmmmmm.'

'Just Hmmmmm?' said Gambit.

'Well, if you prefer it—Hmmmmm...Hmmmmm.'

Gambit glanced at Purdey. 'He's only given us two Hmmmmms.'

'Must be better than one Hmmmmm.'

Steed got back in the act. 'Hmmmmm.'

Purdey nodded. 'That's three.'

Steed laughed and picked up the invitation again. 'Now is the time for all good men...'

Gambit finished for him. '...to come to the aid of the party.'

'Right.'

Hong Kong Harry sipped noisily at his drink. 'I don't know what's happened to you, Steed. It never used to be like this in the old days.'

'You know how it is, Harry, The younger generation—you've got to let them have some fun sometimes.'

Harry sighed. 'They just can't cut it the way we did.'

By evening, Freddy had been through just about every drawer and piece of paper in the laboratory. Then he heard someone coming towards the laboratory and he went back into his cupboard hiding place.

The Professor was still accompanied by Mr Vann and the former was apologising as they entered. 'I must apologise for the inconvenience, Mr Vann, but we must take suitable precautions.'

As Freddy watched, the Professor went to another cupboard and produced two bags. From each one he produced a clear plastic suit, rather like a spaceman's outfit, a suit that, as he helped Vann into it, covered the man from head to foot. In the head-piece there was a breathing apparatus and, as both men dressed, they looked to Freddy like something out of a space film.

'I am sure you understand the necessity for this, Mr Vann.'
Vann sneered, 'If Midas is all you claim.'
Turner beamed. 'Oh, he is. I promise you he is.'
Turner waddled over to the door and unlocked it with some difficulty, before calling down the corridor. 'Midas... Midas.'

Both men and their unsuspected gatecrasher watched as the door at the far end of the corridor opened and the occupant came in. A long, deep red skirt swept right to the ground, rustling as it moved forward, making what to Freddy was a faintly eerie sound. The top half of the body was hidden from Freddy's view as it swished through the laboratory and the two men in their clear plastic suits went after the systerious 'Midas.'

After a while, the building was silent and Freddy once more came out of his cupboard. His first trip was back to Turner's office, where he helped himself liberally to the whiskey decanter. He had not eaten all day, so the drink managed to sustain him.

He also felt that he was missing something. He had been most of the day on his search. He braced himself and went back to the laboratory to start afresh. He would find the facts he needed to put him back right with Steed and the Department if it took another day and another night.

For his experiment, Turner had picked a grand fancy-dress party at a large country house. It was a party that had taken a long time in preparation and no expense had been spared to provide all the guests with whatever they required in the way of costumes. The house was crammed and the party was swinging right from the front door.

Inside the front hall was a broad staircase, curving away to the darkness of the first-floor landing. What appeared to be a Zulu chief was holding court at the bottom of the stairs. He was hot and had been drinking heavily and as he wiped his forehead some of the black came away to reveal that he was a white man in a black face. Near by a white-faced clown was suffering from over-indulgence in the same way, but the wipe of his forehead produced black skin underneath.

Most of the costumes were bizarre, but modern. There were no historical characters here—no Marie Antoinettes or Queen Elizabeth the Firsts.

There was a cat girl, her suit so close-fitting that it looked like an extra skin; a superman—well, actually there were two but one of them was unconscious already on the terrace—a number of women in men's costumes including at least three transvestite versions of Fred Astaire in white tie, top hat and tails. The only unoriginal note was struck by the disc-jockey who was filling the whole house with a blast of sound—he was dressed as a jockey.

He hollered loudly as Barbarella swung by with the Mad Hatter. He was even more pleased to catch sight of a girl pirate in slashed blouse, tight trousers and jack boots. Up by the drinks table Donald Duck had to hold his beak open with both hands before he could pour a drink down himself.

A twenties flapper wearing a mask that gave her a Kewpie Doll face fixed in a permanent rosebud smile, swung across to the disc jockey, tassled skirt and beads swinging.

The party was well underway and the front door was opened to admit three newcomers: two spacemen and a man in the long red robes of the Wizard Merlin—or the Devil. The three newcomers strolled unconcernedly through the racket round them and made for the bar. Most of the drinks were being taken from a huge bowl of punch and, as the others looked round to see who was watching, the Devil let his hand fall into the punch and stirred it for a moment with long fingers. Then he and his two friends turned and slowly made their way back through the house to the front door. In five minutes they were gone—leaving their mark behind them.

It was nearly an hour later that Gambit finally showed up at the party. He was dressed conventionally in dinner jacket and bow tie. As he came up the drive the whole house was a blaze of light, but there seemed to be something wrong, something that he could not understand until he found a parking place and switched off his engine.

It was then that he was struck by an eerie and almost physical wave of silence. He got out of the car and felt almost afraid as he heard his own footsteps crunch across the gravel to the front door—open wide, the light streaming out as if in welcome. But it was a silent and frightening welcome.

Inside the front hall was the Zulu chief but he was still now, sitting on the stairs as if frozen by some terrible force; the clown near by, lying on the floor, for ever indifferent to the colour of his face make-up. Gambit moved cautiously through to the other rooms and the picture was just the same. Everybody present was either unconscious or dead, still in their weird costumes—the Donald Duck figure was lying forward, kept up from the floor by the size of the beak he wore.

Gambit felt some terrible premonition and did not touch any of them. Then, as he was moving back to the hall, his eyes searching round for a telephone, he heard a groan. He went in the direction of the sound and found the twenties flapper moving slightly, one hand fluttering as she groaned. He bent down to her and ripped the mask off her face—the mask that was so clean, the Kewpie Doll smile on the face. Underneath, the picture was a shocking contrast, the face of the girl was the face of death. It was a strange blue-black colour—with here and there livid blotches of purple.

Her eyes widened and she stared up at Gambit for a moment, tried to talk, then slowly relaxed, her eyes rolling up in her head as the death rattle came from her throat.

Gambit laid her down and proceeded to rip the masks from some of the other party-goers. They revealed the same blue-black colouring, the same purple blotches—but they were already dead.

He was still hunting for the phone when he heard a sound in the drive. Instinctively he ducked down—if it was a new guest, he could come out and warn them away. Something told him that the noise meant a new danger and he watched with amazement as two men dressed rather like spacemen helped a third man in long robes down from a Land-Rover in the drive. As the third man turned to face the door, Gambit gasped. The man had the face of a skull, a luminous skeletonic mask that shone eerily in the darkness of the driveway.

The two men in their clear plastic envelopes came in just behind the third mysterious figure. They looked round the hall, then looked in at a couple of the downstairs rooms. One of the spacemen turned to the other.

'You are satisfied?'

'Yes, Professor, I am satisfied. It is worth everything I have promised to you.'

The man who had asked the original question said, 'Come on, let's go back to the labs.'

The three of them turned and swept out of the house, unaware of Gambit's presence. He went cautiously to the front door and watched them climbing back into the Land-Rover. Then he set about trying to find the telephone once more.

Professor Turner, Mr Vann and the strange figure with them made their journey back from the house of death in silence.

It was as they entered the laboratory, that Professor Turner turned to Mr Vann. 'Well—an impressive demonstration of our powers, I think? You are satisfied?'

Vann nodded slowly, encumbered by the clear plastic envelope in which precautions were forcing him to move. 'Fantastic, astonishing.'

Turner beamed. 'Scientific endeavour...It is merely an advance in medicine, nothing more than that. We will show you.'

He turned to the silent figure between them, the figure of death in his long crimson robes. 'Let us show him, Midas.'

The hands, with their long fingernails, came up slowly to the mask that covered his face. As he went to remove it, Vann stepped backwards, frightened of what might greet his eyes, what evil had marked itself so terribly on this living death's face that made it necessary to cover it up.

The face that was revealed as the mask slipped away gave him an even greater shock than he had expected, for Midas was not some twisted, diseased creature, but a literally beautiful young man of about twenty-six, a young Adonis, almost too handsome to be real.

Vann whistled. 'Incredible—his face is entirely un-blemished—is it safe?'

'Yes, as long as you are wearing protective clothing. Here, put on this gauntlet.'

Vann slipped a clear, plastic gauntlet over the covering that was already over his right hand. Then he reached up and tentatively touched Midas on the cheek.

'Incredible—But why would he ... I mean ... Why?'

The young man smiled. 'I trust the Professor.'

'Thank you, Midas, but it is more than that—dross into gold. Mr Vann, when I first encountered Midas he was inevitably doomed—now all that is changed—now I have given him the secret of eternal youth—a fair exchange, I'd say. All right, Midas?'

The young man smiled and turned away. He had a key to the locked door at the end of the laboratory and now he went to it, unlocked the door and, with a backwards smile of acknowledge-ment to Vann, he went through, closing the door behind him.

As soon as the door was closed, Turner said, 'Let's get changed.'

They began, then Turner said, 'I forgot. You touched him with that gauntlet on your right hand, didn't you?'

Vann nodded and the Professor led him over to a bin that was marked: DANGER—CONTAMINATED.

He opened it, stripped Vann's glove off for him and dropped it into the bin. Then the two men finished their changing, shucking off the plastic envelopes—which the Professor gathered carefully from the floor and placed into the same bin.

'In a few moments they will be destroyed and there will be no chance at all of contamination.'

Vann nodded and they moved towards the door of the

laboratory. Professor Turner, buoyed up by the success of the experiment, beamed on his visitor.

'Mr Vann—let us go and talk about gold.'

After they had changed the door closed on them and once more the laboratory was empty. When the silence had lasted long enough for Freddy to believe it was safe to emerge, he did so. His hands were shaking again, but not from deprivation of alcohol this time. What he had learned had made him very frightened. A man whose touch meant death—that was perhaps enough to tell Steed, combined with the other things he had witnessed. Now he knew what papers he was looking for in the laboratory and he started going through the drawers once more, reinspecting papers he had discarded for the concrete evidence he would need for the Department.

After Gambit had been sent off to attend his party, Purdey and Steed kept Hong Kong Harry company, but nothing would change his story. He was just hired as a courier for interests he did not know—nor cared about that much—to transport the gold to England. Eventually all three of them got bored with the circular nature of the questions and answers that went on and Purdey retired to get some sleep. She instinctively thought that the mystery was hotting up and she might get little chance to sleep regular hours.

It was shortly after she had gone that the phone rang. Steed grinned at the voice he heard.

'Why, Madame Sing. This is a surprise. Yes, he's here.'

He handed the phone over to Harry, who took it with some embarrassment, listened for a moment, then breathed a sigh of relief as he replaced the receiver. 'Honest, Steed, I didn't know that they were behind it.'

Steed shook his head. 'Come now, Harry. We get a call from Madame Sing—the head of European operations for the People's Republic of China—and you say that you didn't know you were working for her.'

'Honest,' bleated Harry. 'She can tell you herself when she comes.'

Steed stiffened. 'She's coming here?'

'Yes. That's what she rang for. I wasn't to worry, she was

coming to collect me, couldn't apologise enough for what happened. Said she was looking forward to seeing you again.'

'As long as it's just a friendly visit, I'll be happy to see her too.'

He reached across the desk and pressed a switch on the intercom that was there and could connect him with all the other main rooms in the house. After a while, Purdey answered with irritation. 'What is it now?'

'We're going to have a visitor, Purdey.'

'Well, it had better be someone important. I've had hardly any sleep.'

'Madame Sing.'

There was a long silence the other end, then Purdey said, 'I'm on my way.'

He snapped off the intercom and beamed at the sweating Harry.

'She seems to think that Madame Sing is pretty important too.'

Purdey was down in less than five minutes and together the three of them waited for the arrival of their visitor. It wasn't long before the front doorbell rang. Steed got up and went to the front door to let Madame Sing in. On the doorstep was an incredibly beautiful Chinese girl, dressed in the traditional silk dress with the slit right up to the thigh. Behind her, in the drive, stood her car. It seemed to be empty. She smiled as she bowed to Steed. 'It is all right, Mr Steed. I have come on my own. Hong Kong Harry has been a good friend to us.'

He stepped aside to usher her into the house and she gave a pretty little frown. 'By the way, do you know that there is a large kitchen knife sticking in your front door?'

Steed sighed, reached forward and pulled it out. It was becoming a little too much of a talking point. 'Thank you.'

They re-entered the study. Madame Sing bowed to Purdey and smiled warmly on Harry, who sank back in his chair and mopped his brow, relieved to get a smile out of her. When Steed was seated back at his desk, she said, 'We are very much indebted to you, Mr Steed. An unfortunate affair that you have handled most fortunately, with tact and discretion—and you have taken care of our Mr Hareet most excellently.'

'Well, I've always had a soft spot for Hong Kong Harry—I

suppose it's because he's more scrutable than most.'

Harry rose, not sure whether to take this as a compliment or an insult. 'Thanks again, Steed.'

'We will bid you goodbye, then, Mr Steed,' said Madame Sing.

Steed nodded, smiling broadly. He would dearly have liked to ask questions about the gold transaction, but there was protocol involved here that he could not cut across. He knew from the attitude of Madame Sing that whatever the gold had been intended for, the whole scheme had been aborted now. She would not go on with it now that the British authorities knew that something was going on. There had been too much co-operation of late between the two countries, mainly in Hong Kong.

Madame Sing coughed delicately. 'There is the small matter of Mr Hareet's merchandise...'

Steed grinned. 'Oh, yes.'

He had packed the bags of gold, plus the plastic bag he had collected at the airport, into a large suitcase which he had secreted in the knee hole of his desk. Now he pulled it out with some difficulty.

'Shall I put it in the boot of the car for you?'

'It is all right. I can manage.'

'Well, I've never argued with a lady.'

He handed the suitcase over to her and she took it from him, holding it as if it were as light as a feather. For a delicate little flower she had the strength of steel.

At the door she turned again, and, without putting it down, she bowed.

'Thank you again, Mr Steed. May you have the blessing of many sons to make your old age a tranquil one.'

Steed bowed in return, the smile still on his lips. 'In view of the fact that I am not married, Madame Sing—many sons might prove to be something of an embarrassment—unless, of course, you were going to be personally involved in such an event.'

The lady managed a smile and this time her eyes were laughing too. 'It is a matter of regret that pressing events make it impossible for me to respond to so attractive an offer, but, au revoir.'

Then she was gone, taking Hong Kong Harry with her. Steed subsided behind the desk, a frown on his brow. Purdey uncurled herself from the sofa and laughed.

'Steed, you're becoming a roué.'

'Merely an optimist.' He fell silent, then, 'Damn. I wish something would break on this thing. Something big is happening and we're just on the edges of it.'

As if a prayer were being answered the phone shrilled out. Steed picked it up absently. He was expecting a call from Gambit—they had not heard from him since he had gone out to the party.

'Gambit?'

'It's Freddy.'

Steed managed, 'Freddy. What can I do for you?'

He put his hand over the mouthpiece and filled in Purdey as to Freddy's present condition and the circumstances in which he had run into him only the night before.

On the other end of the phone, Freddy was saying, 'I've got something for you. You're going to have to put that good word in for me now.'

'Is this some sort of joke?'

In the near darkness at the wall phone in Professor Turner's hidden laboratory, Freddy looked at the file he had in his hand—the file marked MIDAS, and replied patiently, 'Oh no, Steed. Freddy the deadbeat is back from the dead—Freddy who got tossed out on his ear will have the red carpet rolled out for him now.'

Steed sighed. This was not the time for comforting the man in a bout of drunken self-pity. 'Freddy, are you on some kind of bender?'

The other man snarled down the line, 'I'm not drunk now, Steed. Intoxicated with power, perhaps, but I'm certainly not drunk.'

'Freddy, it's very late and I—'

Steed was cut off in mid-flow as Freddy said one word, 'Midas.'

'What?'

'I said Midas, Steed. The Midas touch.'

Steed was completely alert now and Purdey leaned forward

to try to catch the words on the phone, seeing the intense expression that had come over his face.

The voice on the other end of the phone went on. 'I can guess that grabs you, old boy.'

Steed tried to suppress the excitement in his voice. 'What do you know about Midas?'

On his end of the phone, Freddy was concentrating too hard on getting his message across, the message that would reinstate him in the Department, to see that the locked door at the far end of the laboratory was slowly opening. He said, 'I know enough, Steed. I haven't lost my touch after all. I saw an old face from Pilton Down—followed it up—and I've struck gold.'

Steed's voice came tensely down the wire. 'Freddy, this is important—'

'You're telling me.'

The door at the end of the laboratory reclosed quietly and the figure that had slipped through came quietly across the darkened laboratory.

'Where are you now? When can we meet?'

Freddy, having got Steed's full attention, said with a growing confidence, 'I'm calling the tune now, old boy. I'll meet you at dawn. At the usual place—just like the old days, eh?'

Steed tried to ask another question, but the line had gone dead. Freddy replaced the receiver, tapped it triumphantly and, smiling, turned to confront Midas himself.

Freddy felt his legs go weak beneath him. But the instincts of his training had not entirely deserted him. He came up with a hard right cross and hit the other man square on the jaw— sending him flying across the room to crash into the far wall, noisily shattering some scientific instruments on the way.

Before Midas had time to recover, Freddy had leaped for the window that he had let himself in by, had lifted it and jumped through on to the fire-escape beyond. He plunged in panic to the ground and skirted the edge of the building. He knew that it would not be many minutes before he was hunted down as the guinea-pig had been hunted down on the building site that was his present home. He had to find some quick means of escape.

He came round the edge of the building and saw that some cars were parked in the area in front of him. In the darkness he almost doubled up as he tried the first door-handle. The car was locked so he tried the next. This one opened to his touch and he climbed in.

There was no key in the ignition, but this was something that did not bother a man who had had Freddy's espionage training. It was the work of a moment to pull down the ignition wires and splice them so that the car roared into life. A moment later he had backed out of the space and was roaring towards the dock gates. So far no one had made any attempt to follow him and he congratulated himself on his quick wits as he crashed through the gates and turned the car through the maze of tiny streets that would lead him out of London and to his meeting with Steed.

Inside the laboratory, the lights were on as Turner and Vann dashed in, disturbed during their negotiations in Turner's office. Midas was at the far end of the room, picking himself up, rubbing his jaw gingerly. The Professor and his guest stopped, keeping their distance from him.

'What happened?'

Midas shook his head to clear it. The blow had been a hard one. 'I'm not sure—an intruder—a burglar, I think...'

Vann was alarmed that security should be so lax. 'What?'

He tugged a gun out from under his jacket and moved over to the window to look down into the darkness beyond. Midas chuckled. 'Don't worry.'

The Professor turned to him. 'You touched him?'

The other man shook his head, but he was still smiling. 'Not exactly. He hit me. A brief touch—but he did hit me. With his bare fist.'

Vann let his jaw drop. 'You mean, as brief a touch as that— that can cause death?'

Turner nodded. 'Perhaps, Mr Vann, we have given you a better demonstration than the party provided—if only we can find the man's body.'

A moment later, they heard the car roar away and the Professor swore. Vann said, 'That spoils your demonstration.'

'Only to the extent that others may find the body first if we do not know where the man will die—but he will most assuredly die...'

• • •

At Steed's home, he had told Purdey the whole story of Freddy's disgrace and dismissal from the Department. Now he rose wearily and said, 'We'd better get a little sleep. We're meeting him at dawn. I'll wake you an hour before.'

'Where are we meeting?'

'He said the old place. That means Meldown Quarry. It's not too far from here. If a bit chilly and melodramatic at that time in the morning.'

Steed had, however, hardly got into bed before the telephone rang. It was Gambit on the line. Steed, in spite of his irritation at being disturbed, managed, 'How was the party?'

Gambit snorted. 'How is it, you mean? It's more like a wake.'

'Well, you can't win them all. Some parties go well, other's don't.'

'Well, this one had just gone. Everybody's dead.'

Steed was wide awake at once. 'Call the police and doctors. Don't touch anything, understand.'

Gambit snorted again. 'What do you take me for?'

Steed breathed a sigh of relief. 'All right—and you'd better stand by there for their reports. I'll see you in the morning.'

'Has anything broken yet?'

'Not yet, but it might have by the time I see you. I've got an appointment with Freddy. It appears that the old drunk knows something about Midas.'

'Freddy? Is it for real?'

'Well, he seems to think it's enough to get him back into the Department, so it may be just what we need. Goodnight.'

Chapter Ten

Steed and Purdey were on the road for Meldown Quarry well before dawn. Even so, Freddy was there waiting for them. He had driven straight from the docks area to keep his appointment, with one side visit to a cache of liquor that he had hidden on a building site similar to the one on which he now lived, and where he had seen Professor Turner and his men go to work.

Freddy had driven the stolen car to the far side of the quarry from the entrance road and had parked it atop the quarry so that, sitting in it, he had a good view of the whole area below. He was not feeling very well and put this down, at first, to the heavy work-load he had got through and the fact of the strain that a day's hiding in the Professor's laboratory had done to his nerves.

As the dawn came it allowed him to pick out the well-remembered features of the abandoned quarry and its workings—the deep pits—the slag heaps, some of them connected by high wooden bridges and the old rusted railway line in the depths of the quarry, still with rusting trucks and stone hods on the useless track.

Where Freddy had parked, the ground sloped forward and a narrow, frail wooden bridge led to the high ground on the other side of the neck of the quarry workings.

Freddy raised a bottle of whisky to his lips and took the last dregs from it. Then he got out of the car and threw the bottle down so that it smashed on the old workings below. It was nearly completely light now and he was getting nervous and impatient for Steed's arrival.

He glanced at his watch and turned back to the car. Opening the door, he stretched his right hand to the back seat to pick up a new bottle of his precious and dwindling stock, then froze in horror. He saw that the whole of the back of his hand was covered in black and blue marks, some of them turning purple almost in front of his eyes. It took a moment for the import of this alarming development to sink in, then he was scrabbling at his jacket and shirt, pulling the shirt apart to inspect his chest.

It was as he feared. The blue-black and purple blotches were on his chest as well. He scrabbled in the car for the file he had found and read through some of the notes again. They told him that the punch he had thrown at Midas in order to escape had been the movement that killed him. The merest touch of Midas meant death.

Even as he was accustoming himself to his fate, he heard the faint sound of an approaching car. He thought at once that it would be Steed and pulled himself back out of his own machine to greet him. Then the full horror of his situation dawned on him. He could not go near Steed—could not even dare hand him the file now that he had touched it.

The sound of the car grew louder and he spun round to see that the vehicle was climbing to the lip of the quarry on the far side. That, at least, was a relief, it might give him time to warn his former colleague not to approach before it was too late.

Steed was driving the car, Purdey at his side. As they bumped close to the edge of the quarry Purdey stirred herself and pointed to the far side.

'There he is.'

The man was standing beside his car, unmoving, staring at them. Steed hooted his horn, playing out a tattoo.

The sound floated over to Freddy as he stood rooted to the spot in his fear. He tried to think what he might do as he saw the car come to a final halt and he watched the driver and passenger climb down. He peered forward and was relieved to see that one of them was Steed—trust him to come to such a secret meeting with a pretty girl.

Steed and Purdey moved forward to the edge of the pit—from where they stared across at the still-unmoving Freddy. They exchanged a puzzled glance at the sight of him, standing there so still. Steed called out, 'Freddy?'

Still the other man made no move and Steed called again, 'Freddy?'

Still the man on the far side of the ravine did not, or would not, move to show recognition. Steed was more than puzzled. He was suddenly afraid. Perhaps it was part of an elaborate trap. He glanced round, but the dawn countryside seemed still and clear.

'Freddy. What's wrong?'

The man held up his hand and stared at it again. He was a dead man, he knew it for sure and there was nothing he could do about it. But Steed did not have to die as well for his mistake. He had been stupid to think that he could get back into the Department, he was stupid to have tried. He made a great effort and snapped himself out of his shock.

'Stay where you are, Steed—don't come any closer.'

His voice was choked and unsteady and was carried away on the light dawn breeze. Steed turned to Purdey, his look asking if she had caught the words and she shook her head in a silent reply. He took another pace forward and shouted out, 'What did you say? I didn't quite catch it.'

Freddy backed away a pace beside the car as Steed took his step forward. He shouted again, 'Stay where you are—for God's sake, Steed.'

Steed and Purdey both turned and made briskly for the frail bridge that crossed the ravine. Freddy slammed back into the car and screamed, 'Steed, you must keep away from me, you must.'

They had reached the footbridge, and now stopped on the far side while they judged whether it would be strong enough to hold them on the way across. Steed said softly, out of the corner of his mouth, 'He must be drunk.'

'Do you think he really knows anything?'

'He knew the name. He must know something. We've got to try and get across to him.'

He put one hand on the edge of the stanchion that led on to the little footbridge. It moved and creaked as he held it. If they raced across, it would be a near thing. Steed called across to the stricken man, 'You called me, Freddy. There must have been a reason. I'm going to come across.'

Steed took a first careful step out on to the bridge. It creaked ominously and he almost stepped back. It was Freddy's next words that gave him the stomach to go on. 'Don't come across. You must stay away from me—I may kill you if you come near me.'

Steed said, 'He must be drunk. We'll have to take him in a rush.'

Purdey nodded and prepared herself to follow Steed across the bridge, like a shadow, as fast as she could. Steed tried to put the other man in a less-panicky mood. 'Not me, Freddy. You wouldn't kill me—we're old friends—we've been through too much together, remember?'

Freddy was almost gibbering with panic. There seemed no way that he could get his message across to the man and girl on the far side of the bridge.

'Steed, no—please don't come.'

'We want to know what you know about Midas.'

Freddy resorted to a desperate bargain. 'Stay on the other side and I will tell you.'

Steed and Purdey were almost half way across. Steed turned and glanced at the girl and she nodded at the look on his face. They were confronted with a confused drunk and the only thing to do was to humour him. Steed shouted across the remaining feet of the space. 'I can't hear you, Freddy. We'll have to come closer.'

He turned to Purdey. 'Get ready to sprint and grab him.'

He turned and shouted once more to Freddy, 'Don't worry, we just have to get closer—just a little closer, that's all. Everything's going to be all right.'

They were almost at the end of the bridge now, just about ready to make their run for Freddy. Steed lowered his voice a little and tried to talk soothingly, 'You don't have to be frightened of me, Freddy. I'm your old friend, John Steed.'

Freddy exploded with bitter laughter. His behaviour seemed to be becoming more and more erratic. 'Me, frightened of you—that's rich—it's the other way around now—the boot is on the other foot.'

Steed said to Purdey, 'Go.'

Purdey sprinted off the bridge and rushed up towards Freddy. He screamed, 'Stay away, I tell you, damn you. Stay away.'

The car was between him and Purdey and she would lose precious seconds going round it to grab the man. Quickly he wrenched open the door and sprang inside. He touched the improvised starter and the car roared into life. Purdey's terrific sprint brought her to the car just as it started to move forward to the edge of the ravine.

She grabbed the handle on the passenger side and clung on. Freddy leaned across, opened the door, then slammed it. The impact knocked her away so that she rolled over and over on the grass. As she got to her feet, Freddy managed to engage gear and drove straight for the edge of the pit.

Purdey rejoined Steed as he rushed forward, but they could only watch in horror as the car plunged over the edge and down to the workings below. They watched as the car smashed against the workings, then they stepped back as there came a huge explosion and the car burst into flames.

They went to the edge of the pit and looked down to Freddy's funeral pyre. Purdey noticed that Steed was human enough to remove his bowler hat for a moment, though he quickly replaced it when he saw that she had noticed it. He sighed and turned away.

'That's that.'

Purdey frowned as they went back across the bridge, which was creaking even more alarmingly than it had on the way across.

'We'll never know the information that he had for us—we're in another dead end. What do we do now?'

Steed had reached the end of the bridge and he turned back to help her.

'We'll just have to wait to see if Gambit has anything to report.'

They went back to the house and further puzzling over what Freddy had said to them—both to Steed on the phone and when he was shouting across the quarry at them. They had been mulling the conversation over for some time when Steed strode across to one of the shelves in his study and produced a small printed book.

'What's that?' asked Purdey.

'On the telephone, Freddy said something about Pilton Down. I'm trying to find someone who was on security there.'

'Was Freddy?'

'He went down from the Department to advise them at one time. His closest opposite number should be somewhere on this list—got it.'

He peered at the name, then handed the book to Purdey. 'Go and see him. He's quite fun actually.'

'Pilton Down's closed. What's he doing now?'

'He's training commandos for the SAS.'

Purdey smiled. 'Thanks. I get all the fun jobs.'

At that moment, Gambit was engaged in a job that he found less than tasteful. The whole country house had been roped off as a proscribed area and the only living beings inside the compound besides himself were doctors and medical orderlies. Even the police had been ordered to stay outside for the moment—their closest duty was to guard the entrance to the restricted area.

Gambit was amazed to watch the medical orderlies at work. They all wore masks and rubber gloves and they were carefully wrapping each of the dead guests and their accessories in plastic sheeting.

One of the senior medical men came up to him. 'We've nearly finished wrapping them all up—found another two in one of the bedrooms upstairs. What a way to go.'

Gambit had been supplied with his own sterile equipment and his eyes glared the man's joke down. The doctor said, 'Are you absolutely sure that you didn't touch any of them?'

Gambit frowned as he tried to remember. 'I don't think so—I pulled off a face mask—I turned another of them over.'

The doctor pressed, anxious. 'But you're absolutely sure that you didn't touch any of them—I mean come into contact with bare flesh?'

'No.'

A nurse had come up and, at the doctor's signal, she grabbed Gambit's shirt-sleeve, undid the cuff and began to roll it up. Gambit pulled away his arm and protested, 'Hey, what are you doing?'

'Just to be on the safe side,' said the doctor. 'An injection. It could just make sure.'

The nurse was allowed to finish her job and jabbed a needle into Gambit's arm. He winced with pain—it was worse than getting a bullet-wound in a fight.

The doctor went on, 'One never knows, does one? It's better to be safe than sorry.'

Gambit rolled down his own sleeve. 'What went on here?'

'I thought that you might be able to tell me—at the moment all we know for sure is that a lot of people have ended up very, very dead.'

'Yes—but the question is how. What did they die of?'

The doctor exchanged a glance with the nurse who had injected Gambit's arm. 'Take your pick.'

Gambit could only stare as the implications of the remark sank home. After a moment, the doctor went on, consulting some notes he had made.

'Of necessity, in the time and under the circumstances, our tests have only been preliminary, you understand. So far it appears that these people died of typhus, typhoid, malaria, pneumonia, small pox, black water fever and beri beri, to name but a few diseases that we've recognised so far.'

'You mean they died of all these things?'

'Most of them died of just one. Most of them would. But each of them died of the disease that they would have been most prone to in the outside world. It was like a great hothouse for epidemics. But, put more simply, yes, Mr Gambit. They died of everything.'

In Professor Turner's laboratory, a strange meeting was taking place, a meeting that would seal the bargain between himself and Mr Vann and get him all the gold he could ever have wished for. Midas attended that meeting, coming, for convenience in his own protective plastic sheeting.

As he entered the room, Vann said, 'Let's make this quick. I have an appointment.'

The Professor raised his hands. 'Patience, Mr Vann—ah, here is Midas now.'

He greeted his valuable property with a bow which the young man gravely returned, the plastic sheeting crinkling loudly as he did so, bringing a smile to his lips. 'Good morning, gentlemen.'

The Professor said, 'Midas, we are selling your—I mean our services to Mr Vann. And, quite rightly, he has asked that you practise what is required of you—a rehearsal if you like—a rehearsal for the real thing tomorrow.'

So saying, he gestured to another man who stood uncomfortably by the door. He had every right to be uncomfortable, dressed as he was in women's clothing and holding a small bunch of flowers in his hand.

Professor Turner laughed. 'Call this a dress rehearsal.'

The guard stepped forward and proffered a hairy hand. Midas bent low over it and kissed it through the plastic.

Vann nodded. 'That is good—and now I must go. I have some preparations to make—and some rehearsals of my own.'

The Professor bowed. 'Till tomorrow, Mr Vann.'

In spite of the fact that it was not due to open until the following day, the hall where the exhibition of Antiquities was to take place was a hive of activity.

Preceded by her prime minister a few days earlier, the Princess had arrived from South America the evening before and had come to the hall for a rehearsal of the opening ceremony, when she would have to declare the exhibition open and meet all the dignitaries that were assembled for the ceremony. This being the day before, all the exhibits were still covered, the sacking and sheets giving little clue to the wealth that lay beneath them.

Mr Vann stood by the Princess, on her right side, as any good prime minister would do under such circumstances. There was little love lost between the two of them since her accession to the principality some months before, but she knew the advantage of biding her time until she was strong enough to dispense with his services—unaware that he was trying to speed up the process in the opposite direction.

At the moment a line of attendants were filling in for the guests of honour and the Princess was proceeding down the line, raising her arm so that each man might bow low over it and kiss her hand. Garvan, the Princess's security man seconded by the War Office, stood near by in his uniform, adorned with two of the Princess's special decorations. He was almost as bored with the run through as she was herself.

She got to the end of the line and Vann said, 'Your most Royal Highness—I will then escort you towards the main door—away from the honoured guests—and the General here will take you at the door and return you to your car.'

The Princess nodded wanly and tried to smile. 'Thank you, Mr Vann.'

'But Your Royal Highness seems very tired.'

'Yes, I am. If we have rehearsed enough?'

'Of course.'

'Then I shall return to my hotel. Thank you, Mr Prime Minister.'

He bowed low over her. 'Your most Royal Highness.'

Vann and Garvin both bowed low as the Princess was escorted away to her waiting limousine, to be whisked back to the hushed safety of Claridges. Both men relaxed visibly now that she had gone. She might be young and very beautiful but she was a hard woman to please. Garvin loosened his tie and said, 'We might as well run through the security precautions—all right with you?'

Vann nodded. 'All right.'

'Well, we've rigged a device on every door—a gun—a knife—anything metallic and it will register on the device. So unless an assassin is prepared to use his bare hands in a crowd, we should be all right.'

Vann made an effort and laughed. 'Assassin. It seems to me that you see assassins everywhere, my dear General Garvin.'

Garvin looked grim. 'There has been one attempt on her life already. We can't afford to let anything happen to her while she is in London.'

'An attempt that was bungled and slip-shod—and what happened to the would-be assassin? He was torn to pieces by the crowd—the populace is devoted to Her Highness.'

'But we must take care. Her Royal Highness is the last of her line. If she should die ...'

'I am aware of that, General. I am equally aware that any anti-monarchist movement that took her life would be rejected by our people—out of sheer sentiment. At the moment, our greatest enemy is probably the common cold.'

Garvin had started to move away. Now something in the intensity of the man's voice made him turn and stare at the prime minister. But there was nothing sinister in his face.

'Don't frown, General. You can see the truth in what I say. If the Princess dies a natural death—then—and only then—would an anti-monarchist group stand any chance at all.'

Garvin acknowledged the truth of this and looked at his watch.

'I must be going.'

'Time presses. Well, see you in the morning, General.'

He watched as the General walked away to the door. He raised his hands and stared down at them, smiling. 'With his bare hands ... His bare hands.'

Steed was not at home when Gambit arrived. A message said that he had gone over to the stud farm to ride. Gambit walked over to join him. He was amused, as he always was, by the name on the gate that announced that he was entering STEED'S STUD but, suppressing his grin, he walked across the grass to where he could see Steed reining in from a brisk canter. Steed rode up and raised his bowler.

'Tally Ho. What was the result of your party-going? Really, it's impossible to let you go anywhere, the damage you do.'

Gambit shuffled his feet awkwardly. 'Well, you're not going to believe this—but the doctors say they died of everything.'

'They died of everything.' Steed almost fell off his horse.

'Everything. The place was a home for contagious diseases—run riot.'

Steed dismounted. He was thoughtful. 'That could explain why Freddy did what he did.'

162

'Freddy?'

Steed sighed.

'A man who never quite forgot what he had once been—no, it's not a riddle, just an epitaph. He killed himself so that Purdey and I couldn't touch him. I think he had the same trouble that your fellow guests did.'

They walked together back to the house and were sitting quietly in the study restoring their brains and muscles with a drink before they took up the subject again. 'Freddy did say one significant thing—about a face he remembered from Pilton Down.'

'Pilton Down's been closed for six years.'

'Seven, actually. I'm not sad about that as a matter of fact. Germ warfare—it's never seemed, well, sporting, to my way of thinking.'

'Which face did he remember?'

Steed stretched himself out comfortably and poured some more whisky into his glass. 'I'm hoping Purdey will find out.'

'Where is she?'

'She's seeing an old friend of mine—used to be on the army security at Pilton Down.'

Purdey was in fact having a very energetic morning. She had gone to the SAS field-training centre near Salibury Plain and had been directed out to the assault courses on the plain itself. Here she had finally caught up with Henry, Steed's old friend, now a burly instructor. Around him were a dozen would-be commandos in full kit, their faces grimed, waiting to go through the course with him.

He started them off—their first problem was to get across a muddy pit by swinging on ropes—then she put her first question.

He frowned. 'Pilton Down. That place had an administration of over a hundred people. All gone their separate ways now.'

'But you were security officer there Steed tells me. You must have known them all.'

Henry's eyes were on his recruits. 'Certainly—Not that bloody way, man—Sorry, miss. Look, wait here, I have to put these muttonheads through their paces. I won't be long.'

So saying, he swung away on a rope. Purdey remained alone

at the end of the course—but not for long. Her face toughened, then she too grabbed one of the swinging ropes and launched herself out over the pit.

The next part of the course was to walk along a thin bar over a large pit and Purdey caught up with him there. He nearly fell off as she said, from just behind him, 'Pilton Down was a big barrel of apples—any rotten ones among them?'

'Of course not. Everyone had complete security clearance— watch out.' This last was to one of the recruits who was in danger of falling off. He then turned to Purdey. 'Please, miss, this is no place for you. We can talk afterwards.'

She shrugged off the misplaced gallantry. 'Don't worry about me. I can take care of myself.'

So saying and, with a movement he could not quite remember afterwards, she got round him on the pole and was suddenly ahead of him. He stared at her as she managed to get to the other side and almost fell off the pole himself in his surprise. She laughed and called back at him, 'Where would you prefer me to be—at the kitchen sink—attending the nursery—or in bed?'

He would have preferred the latter, but somehow didn't think that this was quite the right moment to say so. Instead he said, 'Okay, you win. Let's get on with it. What was it you wanted to know?'

The next part of the course consisted of sliding through huge drainpipes on their stomachs and, as she dived in ahead of him, Purdey asked, 'Was there anyone you were ever suspicious of?'

He was thoughtful as he started into the drain. By the time he was half way through, he said, 'Well, there were a few eccentrics, of course.'

'Eccentrics?'

'You know—oddballs.'

'Odd?'

Purdey came out of the end of the pipe and did a somersault that landed her on her feet. 'In what way?'

As she spoke she began climbing a great net that led to a slippery pole. Henry started after her. 'Quirky ones. Obsessed with their work—careful, lad.' This latter was said to a recruit as he fell past them off the pole to the ground. 'This is a dangerous one, miss. Be careful.' Breathing heavily from the effort, he reached the tenuous security of the pole at the top, then reacted with astonishment bordering on bad temper as he saw that Purdey was at his side with no trouble at all.

'Were they all obsessed with their work?'

'Well—scientific chappies—always obsessed with something—wine—food—promotion—lack of promotion—bigger offices—more equipment—even gold . . .'

Purdey tried not to let too much excitement show. 'Gold?' For once it was she who almost lost her balance.

'Oh, that one,' said Henry. 'Well, he was an extreme case. Old Goldamania, we used to call him—some said that he used to go chasing rainbows—to find the crock of gold at the end, you know.'

Purdey asked carefully, 'Who was he?'

Henry only had to think for a moment. 'Professor Turner. Rum one. Strictly in it for the cash—cash that he immediately turned into gold—he was almost crazy for gold, no doubt about that.'

That was, in the end, all the information that Purdey was able to get and she went back to her little sports car to drive back into town. She would have to set about finding Professor Turner. It was here that she had some luck—perhaps too much.

On the way into town she stopped off for a snack lunch and bought a copy of *The Times* to read with the meal. She opened it and, on page two, she saw the advertisement for the following day's opening of the Golden Antiquities Exhibition. That looked like as good a place as any to begin her search. In the meantime she reported to Steed.

'Any news?' he asked.

'I think that Professor Turner is our man. I know what he looks like, but that's just about all. There's been no trace of him since he left Pilton Down.'

'Where are you now, and what are you doing?'

Purdey laughed. 'Vibrating—having lunch—and getting myself a lucky break, I hope.'

'What do you mean?'

'I told you, Turner's crazy for gold.'

'What's that put you on to?'

Purdey snorted. 'Just look at the ad on page two of your *Times*.'

She put down the phone before Steed had time to question her further. With every moment that passed she was becoming more sure that she was on the right track.

Purdey's pass was enough to get her past the guards and into the exhibition hall where everything was being prepared for the grand opening the following morning. She had been there only a few minutes when a Range-Rover pulled into the car park in front of the exhibition hall. Professor Turner got out and went with Simpson, who had driven for him, into the hall.

Inside, she soon saw the most important person present and recognised him from previous press photographs as Mr Vann, the Princess's prime minister. He was arguing with an official as to how far the red carpet should stretch the following morning.

A moment later, she saw Professor Turner enter the room and Vann immediately broke away from the official and went over to him. She moved quickly through the exhibits so as to be in a position to overhear them. Vann said 'You fool. What are you doing—to come here . . .'

Turner looked apologetic but determined. 'I had to come. I had to see—all this. All these shall be mine? That is the bargain, isn't it?'

Vann nodded. 'Yes. But you must go.'

The two men started to walk towards the door. Purdey was about to follow when she felt something hard and cold in her ribs. She turned her head slightly and the man who was pressing the gun into her side smiled. 'My name is Simpson.'

Purdey managed a wan smile. 'How do you do.'

Simpson called, 'Professor.'

Turner and Vann both turned. As soon as they saw Simpson had someone with him they hurried over. Professor Turner smiled at her. 'You'd better come with us, my dear.'

'I don't suppose I have any choice in the matter?'

The Professor shook his head. 'No. I don't suppose you do.'

Steed and Gambit arrived at the exhibition hall almost an hour later. They were relieved to see Purdey's car alone in the car park, but more than a little alarmed when they were unable to find her in the exhibition hall. The curator was showing some people round as they searched through the exhibits and they could hear his voice droning on, 'Of course, this is only a preview of what you will be able to see—tomorrow the exhibition will be formally opened by Her Most Royal Highness...'

Steed and Gambit had made their individual circuits of the exhibits and met again at the main doors. 'She's not here.'

'But her car is.'

They looked at each other grimly. She must have been on to something, right enough—something that had got her kidnapped and in danger. For Steed and Gambit, the situation was hopeless—their only lead was this exhibition.

The Range-Rover came round the side of the apparently deserted docks building and pulled into a parking space next to its companion. Professor Turner had driven them back, Vann beside him. Purdey had been forced to travel in the back, Simpson's gun on her all the way.

Now she was invited to get down and go into the building. She was amazed at the way that the interior had been made over. The ground floor seemed to be a huge reception area, modern and comfortable. Then she went into a lift and was transported to the first floor. She was taken along a corridor and Professor Turner opened a door to let her in. It was his own room and she glanced round at the golden objects that now surrounded her. 'Goldamania.'

Turner smiled. 'Ah. I see you have been checking up on me.'

'Goldamania?'

Turner turned to Vann to explain. 'That is a name they coined for me when I was at Pilton Down. It meant nothing to me. It was coined by soulless fools who could not know the sheer, sensual pleasure of gold. Pure gold.'

He picked up one of the objects and began to caress it as he went on, 'You are very beautiful. Yet, in my eyes, quite worthless in comparison to this one object.'

Purdey sneered, 'I bet it can't cook an omelette—French style—with fine herbs and all the trimmings.'

Turner smiled. She was not going to get a rise out of him by this method. 'A tiny sliver of this will buy me a hundred omelettes—not that the pleasures of the flesh have ever held a great attraction for me.'

Vann thought the conversation had gone far enough. He briskly interrupted. 'What are we going to do with her?'

'Ah, yes. What indeed?'

Vann had a solution of his own—he produced a wicked snub-nosed automatic from his pocket. But Turner shook his head and pushed the gun aside. 'No. I'll have no unnecessary violence—and within a few hours from now we will be gone— you, to a triumph in your own country—me to the foothills of the Andes—they say there is much gold still to be found there.'

Purdey chipped in. 'It didn't do Humphrey Bogart any good.'

They turned and regarded her blankly and she went on, 'The treasure of the Sierra Madre. Most people think that Walter Huston directed it—but it was John.'

As she finished, the door started to open. They all turned towards the newcomer as he shuffled inside—Midas, clothed in his protective shield of plastic. He glanced at Purdey, then turned to Turner. 'I saw her as you brought her in, from the windows in my quarters. She is very beautiful and I am very lonely.'

The import of what he said hung in the air for a moment, when no one moved or spoke, he went on, 'Professor...You promised me...One day...?'

Turner nodded. 'Very well.'

Midas took a step towards Purdey, who stood her ground somehow, did not shrink away. 'Thank you, Professor.'

Turner snapped suddenly, 'After your mission is accomplished.'

Midas hesitated in mid-stride. Then he turned towards the Professor, nodded and went back towards the door. In the doorway, he paused to smile back at Purdey. Then he was gone the way he had come, like something from another planet.

Turner turned to Vann. 'Problem solved. We will give her to Midas—his kisses will be tender and passionate—but very brief...'

Another man, Froggart, came in and Purdey was forced into a chair and tied to it. Then she was carried by Simpson and Froggart to a small room that led off the laboratory and left there. She heard Turner designate Froggart to guard her when they were gone—but for the moment, she was locked in and alone—very much alone. She could only pray that Steed and Gambit would get some clue as to her whereabouts—but she did not see how they could.

Chapter Eleven

Gambit and Steed split up after they had left the exhibition hall. Steed had decided to follow up on the people around the Princess to find, as he put it, 'If he could see a rotten apple in that particular barrel', but Gambit was left very much to his own devices.

There was only one opening they hadn't covered and, for some reason, Steed had not suggested it—Hong Kong Harry and Madame Sing. Gambit did not understand the agreement that Steed seemed to have with Madame Sing, an agreement that came as much out of the protection of Steed's own agents in the Asian area as a respect for Madame Sing's person and protection. Steed knew he could not touch Madame Sing—but he knew also that if they had known anything else of importance, she or Harry would have told him. Gambit knew none of those things.

It was for this reason that he made for the centre of London—the new Chinatown of Gerrard Street and the surrounding streets. Madame Sing had a front as the manager of a news agency and Gambit knew that its offices were to be found in a mews off Gerrard Street itself.

He went inside, pushed past the reception desk and entered

Madame Sing's own room. Her office consisted of a vast open area, with just a desk and two chairs at the far end. Madame Sing was seated at her desk, another Chinese beside her. As Gambit came in, the man rose. He was massive, a vast, shaven-headed Chinaman. Madame Sing's hand was raised, signalling him to stay back.

The receptionist came through the door after Gambit and grabbed him by the shoulder. Gambit threw the man to the floor, where he landed with a crash and lay still.

Madame Sing seemed to be totally unfazed by this sudden turn of events. She smiled across the room. 'Mr Gambit, isn't it?'

Gambit was not interested in the conventions of good manners, whether European or Oriental. 'Where's Hong Kong Harry?'

He strode towards the desk as he spoke, but Madame Sing did not move a muscle. 'I am sorry I cannot help you. Mr Hareet has already departed to other shores.'

'You owe us a favour,' snapped Gambit.

The woman nodded. She knew the value of an obligation. She was, after all, Chinese. 'It is true—I have a small duty to your Mr Steed, but . . .'

Gambit overrode her pretty speech. 'We know that Harry was on his way to barter with a Professor Turner. We know that now. What we don't know is where this barter was to take place—where Turner is. But do you.'

Madame Sing remained impassive. 'Mr Gambit—it is getting late.'

Gambit snarled, 'Very. It's very damned late. Turner has grabbed Purdey—and we want her back.'

Madame Sing rose and sighed. 'It is a reasonable request. If you care to put it through the proper channels.'

'There's no goddamn time for that.'

Madame Sing raised her voice for the first time. 'Goodnight, Mr Gambit.'

'But . . .'

'I said goodnight. I am sorry, but . . .'

Gambit did not move and she signalled with her eyes. The man at Madame Sing's side started to move forward and she said, 'I would prefer it if you left of your own volition.'

When Gambit still did not move she went on, 'I feel I must warn you, Mr Gambit. Choy here is our physical education attaché. An OK Top Class Bodyguard—Grade A.'

Gambit still held his ground. For a moment the man stood in front of him, unmoving also. Madame Sing said, 'Choy.'

Obediently, the man made his move and only then did Gambit retaliate. As the man grabbed him, he went loose, straightened up again and tensed suddenly, then let his elbow perform its tattoo pattern on the man's body. When the action stopped, it was Choy who had ended up in a heap on the floor.

Gambit stood back. 'Grade B.'

Choy groaned and tried to rise, but could not. Gambit snapped, 'Tell him to stay where he is—unless you want this to blow up into an international incident.'

Something flickered across Madame Sing's face. Could it have been fear? No, Gambit could see that she would not want any of this to be reported back to Peking.

She said something in Chinese, then translated, 'Choy. Stay where you are.'

Gambit moved over to the desk and leaned over it. 'Now that we have some sort of understanding, perhaps we can get things straight. Something tells me that we are on the same side in this thing.'

Madame Sing nodded. 'We are not enemies on this.'

'Have you any idea what Midas is?'

Madame Sing shook her head. 'Not in detail—but we know that it is a great danger to the whole world. We wanted to do a deal to suppress it. Your own people and the Americans were not interested—and the Russians, they would have used it on us.'

'So you were going to buy it out to kill it.'

'Yes. Now we have lost our chance.'

'Well, to help you decide if you'll help me, I'll tell you what Midas is. I suppose you've no idea what Turner was working on in Pilton Down?'

Madame Sing smiled. 'No. My predecessor was more interested in the comforts of Britain than in its secrets.'

'Well, he was working on the ultimate in carriers. A healthy rat can carry plague—and can remain immune. The common house-fly can carry a dozen diseases and yet remain unaffected—take that to the ultimate—a man—a human being, scientifically infected with every deadly disease in the book—but not infected himself.'

'Impossible.'

'Not at all, Turner has done it. No signs of infection—every symptom kept at bay and hidden by drugs. A man who could walk into this room, could take your hand—and could kill you just as surely as if he put a bullet into you.'

Madame Sing was staring at him in horror as his voice rose almost to a shout.

'That's what Professor Turner has been working on. That's Midas—now, are you going to help us to find Purdey?'

'I will tell you what I can. It is not much.'

Gambit's voice turned to a plea. He was convinced that the woman was going to be completely frank. 'Please. Anything you can. However little you think it is.'

'All we know is that the Professor has his laboratory somewhere in the London docks.'

'The docks?'

'Yes, by the river near Tower Bridge.'

'But that is a huge area to cover. Do you know how large they are?'

The woman shrugged. 'I have heard they are large enough to swallow up an army. They have certainly swallowed up Professor Turner and his experiments.'

Gambit bent to kiss her hand. 'My thanks, Madame Sing. Now let us see if an army of two can find what an army might lose.'

As Gambit set off to find Steed and make tracks to the docks with him, Purdey was putting her captivity to as much use as the restricted conditions would allow her. In the laboratory beyond where she was imprisoned, tied to her chair, she could hear voices. With infinite patience, she manoeuvred the chair on which she was tied towards the door, then bent down so that she was able to see through the keyhole at least a small part of the laboratory beyond.

The sight that greeted her eyes was, at least at first, more puzzling than enlightening. There was something almost comic about it.

For she could see the guard who had been assigned to look after her the next morning, dressed in women's clothing and holding out a limp hand so that the stranger in the plastic cocoon could bend over and pretend to kiss it—yet another rehearsal on which the Professor had insisted.

Gambit located Steed at his club and the two men drove together to the docks. Steed reported that he had found out little.

'I was having a drink with Jackie Garvin when you arrived—General Garvin. He's in charge of the security for the Princess during her visit and will be running things with that prime minister of hers tomorrow morning. He hasn't come across any rotten apples in her entourage.'

Gambit said, 'Well, I didn't have a drink—I got this information that Turner's hidden himself somewhere at the docks and that's our most likely place to find Purdey.'

Steed snapped, 'Who told you?'

'Madame Sing.'

Steed stiffened. 'You went to her?'

Gambit was ready for a row. 'Yes.'

Steed relaxed. 'Well, you got out alive—and with some information. She must like you—lucky devil.'

They left it at that as the dock gates loomed up. Steed said, 'Park just down the street. All the dock entrances are on this side. If we search we should still stick close to this side so that if any of them leave, we may see them.'

'How long do we wait?'

'Till morning, if necessary. After all, they have to leave for the exhibition if that's where they're going to try out Turner's secret weapon.'

They went into the docks and split up in the darkness to begin their apparently hopeless search. It was an exercise that was to have no result until morning.

Professor Turner led his establishment by being up and about by dawn the next day. Mr Vann had stayed at the laboratory in a suite of rooms overnight, so he was up and ready at the same time as the Professor.

They waited in the laboratory for Midas to come to them. The door opened at last and he waddled in. Beneath the clear plastic covering he was wearing full court outfit including a beautifully fitting cutaway coat. Both men looked at him in admiration for a moment, then Vann said, 'We must hurry if I am to get him inside the hall before the others arrive.'

Professor Turner nodded. 'Come, Midas.'

The two men went with him to the door, then the Professor glanced back. 'Froggart. Keep an eye on the girl.'

The guard grinned. 'It'll be a pleasure.'

Midas turned and said sharply, 'Don't touch her—she's mine.'

The Professor smiled up at him. 'He has his orders.'

As Midas looked round at him, Froggart kept his face straight and nodded confirmation. Then they were gone. As soon as the sound of the lift came to him, Froggart closed the door of the laboratory and unlocked the door to the little room.

Purdey had moved her chair back to the centre of the room and looked up at him, pretending surprise at seeing him, as he entered the room and leered down at her. He moved up very close to her, gun in hand and then moved right round leaning close enough to breathe in her face.

'I can't touch, but they didn't say anything about looking.'

Outside, the Range-Rover with Professor Turner, Midas, Vann and Simpson aboard, moved through the docks at a careful speed. It was Gambit who saw it go by first, and he waited until it was out of sight before walking in the direction from which it had come. He did not know how close he had been. The building they had spent the night looking for was just behind the building from which he had seen the Range-Rover emerge. After circling it and seeing the guard inside the front entrance, he thought that his best point of entry would be through the iron fire-escape at the back. He went round the building again and started to climb it.

Froggart was becoming something of a bore. After walking round her a number of times as if memorising her vital statistics for life, he had now poked the barrel of his machine-gun at her hair to get a better view of her face. It had its compensations for, having heard a noise outside, she was able to see, where the hair had been cleared, that the door of the room was slowly opening. She said, 'Naughty. You're touching.'

'Scared?'

Purdey shook her head and laughed, 'It's all right. I can take it. I've seen ugly faces before.'

Froggart ignored the insult. He was licking his lips. 'It's crazy—wasting you on Midas like this.'

The door was completely open now and she could see Gambit in the doorway, waiting to make his move. It was time she gave him a little more help. She sighed. 'If you did touch me—who'd tell them about it?'

It took the man more than a moment to let this sink in. Then he smiled. 'You're having me on.'

She shook her head. 'Why should I be? I wouldn't tell them.'

'You're kidding.'

Behind him, in the laboratory, Gambit was carefully removing his shoes, ready to make his move. He was unarmed, the other man had a machine-gun. He could not afford that split second of warning. Either of them could die if Froggart got his finger on the trigger for a moment.

Purdey said, 'You don't know what you can do until you try.'

As she looked beyond the leering guard, his mind still only half made up, she saw Gambit begin his run. Quickly she jumped her chair sideways on to the man.

'Untie me—and I'll show whether I'll let you touch me or not, quickly. I want you now.'

Froggart moved forward, his mind made up. At the last moment he sensed something wrong behind him and started to swing round. Gambit still had a couple of yards to go—he finished his run with an instinctive tackle. He hit Froggart and as the machine-gun fell from his hands it chattered out a hail of bullets that thudded into the ceiling.

The noise of them brought Steed at a run towards the building from his portion of the docks.

Froggart hit the wall with a dull thud that put him out of the running for any further part of the proceedings. Gambit snatched up the machine-gun and Purdey, still tied to the chair snapped, 'Gambit. We wanted him awake.'

Gambit shrugged off the reproof. 'Are you okay?'

'Oh, for heaven's sake untie me. You'll be happy to know that I am completely free from infection.'

He untied her, then both of them spun round at the sound of a tremendous crash. They ran into the laboratory, ready for trouble, to see Steed lying on the floor. He had come through the door in such a rush that he had smashed into a table of glass and instruments and had knocked them flying before ending up on the floor himself.

'Better late than never, I suppose,' snapped Gambit.

Steed picked himself up and dusted himself down. He looked only a bit abashed. Gambit tried a bit of cold comfort. 'Never mind, Steed. It was good practice in case you ever get somewhere first.'

Steed did not bother to reply. They walked back into the corridor and only then did he say, 'Don't worry about the other guards. They all seem to be asleep on the job—at least they are now.'

Gambit put a sarcastic hand on Steed's shoulder. 'Well done. You are improving.'

Steed glared at him, then tried the door that led to Professor Turner's office. It swung open and he glanced inside, then stopped and walked in. 'All that glitters is gold—where are they?'

Purdey shook her head. 'They left about an hour ago. I don't know. That guard might have told us—but Mike hit him with one of his haymakers. He might have explained the hand-kissing.'

Gambit frowned. 'Hand-kissing?'

'Yes. They were perfecting it to a fine art.'

'Yes,' said Steed, 'they were rehearsing.'

The others turned to him. 'What's it about, then?'

Steed sighed. 'What do you do when you meet a Princess?'

Gambit shrugged. 'Well—I meet so many.'

But Purdey had got the idea. 'You might kiss her hand.'

• • •

The first of the ticket holders were going into the great hall of the exhibition. Announcements outside said that that day's viewing was by invitation only and that the Princess would open the exhibition at twelve noon.

Prime Minister Vann, suitably dressed for the occasion, was in the great hall. He had been button-holed by the curator, also dressed for the occasion and nervous of the arrangements. Vann was saying, 'Her most Royal Highness will receive the bouquet here, will she not?—And then move into the body of the hall.'

As he spoke he was forced, it was almost a compulsion, to glance round at a huge Golden Sarcophagus that formed one of the exhibits and—standing next to it—Professor Turner.

The curator, excitably, was describing his part in the coming proceedings. 'And then I shall be presented.' He turned to the official photographer who was benefiting from this run-through of the ceremony; 'Be quite sure that you get a good, clear picture. I should so like it on my wall.'

Vann went on, 'Those chosen to be presented will then be lined up here—you will not speak to the Princess unless—or until—she speaks to you.'

The curator nodded and Vann knew from long experience of such people that this was an injunction that he would not obey. Now the man rubbed his hands together. 'Oh, I do so love Royals. There are so few real monarchs left in the world today. And I am given to understand that, even in your lovely country, there is some sort of movement for its overthrow?'

Vann made a vague gesture of dismissal. 'They are just rumours.'

The curator was not to be put off so easily. 'Oh, really. I thought that I read somewhere that they had made an actual assassination attempt?'

Vann turned on the man, white with a combination of anger at his words, and nervousness at the new assassination attempt that could not possibly fail—once Midas had got to the Princess.

'This is hardly a fitting conversation for such an occasion as this.'

The curator had the grace to be abashed. 'Oh, yes, of course. I am sorry—Well, if there's nothing more I can do for the moment . . .?'

'No, there is nothing more.'

The man walked away, affronted by the prime minister's attitude. As he went he comforted himself with the thought that he had read other things as well—for example, that the prime minister was not long for his office, if rumour was anything to go by.

As for Vann, he turned again and met Professor Turner's eye. The latter nodded acknowledgement and his hand brushed against the closed sarcophagus. He looked at the beautiful gold watch on his wrist. In just ten more minutes he would have earned his reward—and own more gold than anyone else in the world.

Gambit and the others were a good deal more than ten minutes' drive away from the hall at that moment. He screamed round a corner, narrowly missing a woman with an overlarge shopping basket.

Purdey said, 'You just missed five points.'

'Never mind. I'll pick it up at the next corner. I see a nun over there.'

A car pulled out of a line of traffic ahead of them. Gambit went through and swerved in front of an oncoming car with seconds to spare. Steed opened his eyes again and said, 'You should take up motor racing.'

'I did once. Daytona, Le Mans, Spa, Monza. Trouble was, I kept crashing at all of them.'

Purdey grimaced. 'It's always nice to know the truth about a fellow worker.'

They roared through a set of red lights and Steed slipped down in the back again. He had shut his eyes but now he took the added precaution of covering his face with his bowler hat.

The Princess's car pulled up outside the exhibition hall. As she came up the steps to be greeted by General Garvin and her prime minister, Mr Vann, the eyes and attention of everyone else in the great room was centred on the door through which she would walk.

This was the moment for which Professor Turner had been waiting. He tapped sharply on the sarcophagus and stepped in front of it. Only someone very close could have noticed that he was wearing rubber gloves—just in case.

The lid of the sarcophagus opened and Midas stepped out, perfectly groomed and perfectly dressed for the presentation. He had stepped forward and was at the end of the line that the Princess had to meet before anyone had noticed anything amiss.

Professor Turner went back to the side of the sarcophagus and closed down the lid. Everything was as it had been before— except for the extra presentee at the end of the line.

The main doors opened and everyone faced ahead as the Princess, accompanied by Prime Minister Vann and General Garvin came into the room. The latter glanced quickly to the end of the line and was both relieved and excited to see that his special, and oh so expensive assassin was in position.

The Royal party had reached the curator and Vann turned and bowed to the Princess in order to present him. 'Now, if Your Royal Highness would graciously consent to meet some honoured guests...'

Her Royal Highness gave the blank smile that indicated that she did give her consent and the curator stepped forward and bowed.

Almost at once, the curator started talking, in spite of a glare from Vann. All the prime minister could do was grit his teeth and wait.

At last, the Princess managed to silence the man and move on to the line of special guests. Vann introduced the first of them, the chairman of the Museum committee.

'May I present Lord Elliston...'

The line seemed interminable, but Gambit and the others were still a good minute away by the time the Princess had progressed to the half-way mark. Six more introductions, six more handshakes and then she would shake hands with death.

The car screamed into the exhibition car park, throwing up a shower of gravel that was going to cost the Rolls-Royce hire company at least three resprays. There was no problem with parking. As the attendants rushed up to intercept them, Gambit brought the car to a sudden halt at the foot of the front steps and he, Purdey and Steed jumped out, almost as one person.

Now there was just one person between the Princess and death. He was a committee member from the group that had mounted the exhibition, slightly deaf, but a garrulous man when invited to speak. In spite of Vann's silent prayer, the Princess asked him how long he had been planning to mount the exhibition. Vann shifted nervously and glanced at Midas, but the latter remained calm and cool, just waiting to carry out his part of the proceedings. On the far side of the room, Professor Turner idly caressed one of the gold objects as he swallowed his own impatience at the delay.

At last, the talk was over and the Princess passed on. Quickly her prime minister said, 'May I present Lord Midas.'

The Princess inclined her head—smiled with genuine pleasure at being able to meet such a handsome young man— and put out her hand.

It was at that moment that pandemonium broke loose at the entrance to the room. Steed, Purdey and Gambit burst through the doors and Steed shouted, 'No.'

The whole Royal receiving line froze for a second like a waxwork tableau.

Steed rushed forward as Midas, the first to recover his power of thought and reason, reached forward for the hand of the Princess as she stood very still before him.

Steed moved forward with a speed that startled even his companions. It wasn't that he couldn't do it, it was just that he couldn't often bring himself to make such an effort. He managed to throw himself forward and sweep the Princess up before anyone else could move to protect her. She crashed to the ground with him, though, being an Englishman, he managed to get underneath to break her fall.

Vann's hand went to his pocket and the little snub-nosed automatic appeared in his hand. Gambit could move quickly too and he was already up with him. His hand chopped down and the gun hit the floor before Vann cried out in pain. Gambit's other hand went fast across Vann's chest, the man's eyes crossed and he sat down heavily—and permanently as far as the mêlée that was breaking out was concerned. Steed was trying to maintain his gallantry under more than difficult circumstances.

'It'll be something to talk about back at the Palace, Your Highness.'

Midas now made his move, away from the line, trying to slip

away. Purdey spotted his move and started to move up on him. Steed shouted in alarm:

'For God's sake, Purdey, don't let him touch you—whatever you do.'

Purdey knew that without having to be told, but she was not ungrateful for the advice. She squared off as the man tried to run towards her, his hands thrust out to touch her. She went up on her points, lifted her leg in an elegant kick and missed her adversary by inches. His hand came past her and she was forced to duck, almost losing her balance.

Behind the fight, Steed was getting to his feet and helping the Princess up and into the hands of General Garvin.

'Take her into the office, she'll be safe there.'

But the Princess smiled. 'I must watch—and thank your friend for what he did. I have always wanted to do that to my prime minister.'

Steed gave her a little bow, acknowledging her courage. Out of the corner of his eye he could see Professor Turner trying to look inconspicuous by the sarcophagus and he started to edge round the side of the small crowd of confused dignitaries to get at him.

Midas had reached the end of the room and was turning again to face Purdey. Once more he moved in, his hands outstretched. Purdey rose to her points again, spun, pirouetting faster and faster, lashing out with one foot as he came to her. This time her shoe caught him in the centre of the chest. He spun round and fell away, his arms flailing.

Turner had seen Steed coming towards him. Now he chose to make his break for the door. His timing could not have been worse. Midas was thrust against him, his hands outstretched. The hand of Midas took Professor Turner full in the face. He screamed and lashed out, thrusting Midas away as he staggered away himself, blind to everything but the reality of the fact that he was already a dead man—killed by his own Frankenstein monster—his own creation. He fell to his knees and began to crawl in circles of tight panic.

As for Midas he regained his balance, turned and made another rush at Purdey. This time, her slippered foot took him under the chin.

He flew backwards across the room towards Steed and the sarcophagus. Steed opened the lid, Midas spun in and Steed let the lid drop on him, before jumping up and sitting on it—just in case Purdey's blow had not been quite hard enough.

The Museum curator came forward, intent on helping the Professor to his feet. With a smile of apology, Gambit stuck out his foot and tripped him up. He fell heavily, but it was his dignity that was hurt more than anything else.

Steed said, 'Nobody is to touch that man.' He turned to Garvin and handed him a card. 'Will you call this number. Ask them to send a medical team. They'll clean everything up here.'

Garvin read the card, then almost saluted Steed before racing off on his mission. Steed himself went over to the Princess. 'Your Highness—is everything satisfactory?'

'Quite satisfactory, thank you. I have not enjoyed myself so much in a long time.'

Turner chose that moment to stop crawling round in circles. He looked up at Steed, his face already showing the results of the Midas touch—black and blue blotches all over his face.

Steed turned the Princess away from the sight and introduced her to Gambit and Purdey. 'When you come to bestow the awards—I'm afraid you'll have to make it three.'

'I will certainly make a note of it.'

General Garvin came back. 'The team is on its way. I'd better get Her Highness out of here before they come.'

Steed nodded, bowed over the lady's hand and kissed it. When she had gone, he turned to the others. 'Let's go.'

'What's happening now? I could do with a rest,' said Purdey.

'Not until we've made out our reports for "Mother".'

Purdey laughed. 'When we've made them out for you, you mean.'

'Well, a boss has to learn to delegate.'

They went down the steps together. The Princess's car was about to drive away, but a traffic warden stood in front of Gambit's machine, together with a policeman who was also taking particulars.

Steed said, 'I know a very nice pub round the corner where we could get a drink until they go away.'

The three of them walked past the car and out of the exhibition car park—together and in step, as they always were. Three bodies and three minds working as one—the New Avengers.

Sit down, relax and read a good book...

CURRENT BESTSELLERS FROM BERKLEY